"How have you been getting on?"

Miranda opened her mouth to make a noncommittal reply but instead blurted out the truth. "Your men don't want me here. You were right. They resent me."

To her dismay she triggered a look she'd seen before on his dark features. Suddenly he seemed ill at ease, slightly guilty. Benvenuto went to the windows and stared absently at the waterway below.

"No," he agreed quietly. "They don't want you here." He swung around on her. "But I do, Miranda. Remember that. *I* want you here, and what I say goes."

She sensed a ruthlessness, a determination behind his high-handed statement, and felt a tremor of alarm. Whatever his reasons for bringing her—a foreigner and a woman—into his craftsmen's domain, falling in love with the boss would only make matters worse.

Liza Manning was born in Lancashire but now lives in the Cotswolds with her husband and the youngest of their three grown sons. An avid reader since childhood, she is now fulfilling a long-standing ambition to write. She is also an enthusiastic cinema- and theatergoer and loves to travel when home and family responsibilities permit. Her research for *The Glass Madonna* took her to Venice, but the people involved with the glassworks there were so secretive that she returned home empty-handed. Luckily, on her return, she discovered a specialist in London's Bond Street, who shared with her a wealth of information.

The Glass Madonna

Liza Manning

Harlequin Books

TORONTO • NEW YORK • LONDON
AMSTERDAM • PARIS • SYDNEY • HAMBURG
STOCKHOLM • ATHENS • TOKYO • MILAN

Original hardcover edition published in 1986
by Mills & Boon Limited

ISBN 0-373-02818-0

Harlequin Romance first edition February 1987

CHAPTER ONE

MIRANDA handed her passport to the official at Marco Polo Airport. The man leaned forward, elbows on his counter, and compared her with her photograph. Shrewd dark eyes studied her delicate English skin; her hair, tumbling wheat-coloured and shining round her shoulders; her eyes, dark blue but at that moment bright with anticipation.

She watched the man's fingers holding the passport, and thought that he seemed in no hurry to return it. Phrases of her newly learned Italian formed in her mind, anticipating his questions, but when he spoke it was in English, slow and deliberate, with one finger tapping the endorsement on the first page. 'You do not come to us for the holiday, Signorina? You come to Venice to *work*?' He sounded surprised and slightly affronted.

'Yes. I'm here as an—an apprentice. A trainee.'

The man eyed her dubiously, as if he doubted whether the craftsmen of Venice would train any foreigner, let alone a female.

Miranda brought out a crested envelope, keeping her movements confident and controlled so he wouldn't guess that this was the first time she'd travelled abroad on her own. 'Here is a letter of authority from Signor dei Santi, who has a factory here. Perhaps you know the name?'

The man read through the letter and looked closely at the signature. 'Ah yes—dei Santi.' He smiled gravely and inclined his head, giving Miranda her first glimpse of the Venetian talent for implying without words that a favour has been bestowed. With a flourish he handed back her passport and the letter.

'Welcome to Venice, Signorina.'

She walked on and stood waiting for her luggage with the other passengers, then grasped her two cases and was nodded through the quiet customs benches. Suddenly, unnervingly, tiredness hit her. It was so unexpected she stopped in her tracks. For goodness' sake, this was no time to feel tired! She was young, radiantly healthy, and on the brink of the most exciting experience of her life.

Admittedly she'd been travelling since six that morning and it was now late afternoon, with her arrival two hours behind schedule because of a delay in taking off from Heathrow. Added to that the flight had been horribly bumpy, especially over the Alps; and the descent disappointing, with that longed-for aerial view of Venice lost beneath low cloud, cloud which had seemed to be at ground-level during a nerve-racking touch-down.

Someone was supposed to be here to meet her. Would they have waited an extra two hours? She stood there as hugs and kisses and greetings in Italian were exchanged all around her. Then she saw a stocky, grey-haired man holding up a card which bore the name: Miss M. Brown. She moved towards him thankfully.

'I'm Miranda Brown,' she said, smiling.

'Signorina!' There was surprise there, quickly concealed as he bent over her hand in a formal little bow. 'Baldassare Gastone Antelami.'

It took seconds for it to register that he was stating his name. 'How do you do,' she replied gravely.

'I come from the establishment dei Santi.' He seemed to have learned his phrases off by heart, because he smiled apologetically as he paused to remember what came next. 'I will take you to your *pensione*. Please to follow me.' He picked up her cases and led her to a motor launch which swayed gently at a landing stage only yards from the airport entrance. All was still, all was grey; grey sky, grey water, and drifting grey mist.

Miranda allowed herself to be tucked away in the cabin, and accepted a rug to go over her knees. Now in peaked cap and waterproofs, her escort edged the boat forward, and she could just make out shallow reed beds on either side. Then they were in open water, where with a roar of the engine the launch leapt forward as if visibility was clear for miles ahead, following a course marked by stout wooden stakes fastened together in threes, pointing tripod-like from the still water.

It was all very different from how she'd imagined it in her daydreams as she walked the winter streets above the river at home. She'd pictured herself in the prow of a boat that purred peacefully across a sparkling lagoon, with the creamy-pink walls of the Doges Palace rising dream-like from the waters ahead of her, while ranked black gondolas dipped at their moorings. Instead of all that she could see nothing at all except the sinister wooden stakes as they sped past them.

She wondered what they would all be doing at home in the neat detached house overlooking the River Stour. Betty, her stepmother, would be getting tea, and Bobby would be into everything with the dynamic energy of the toddler. Then Dad and the boys would come in, ravenously hungry as always . . .

Across the river the Black Country town of Stourley would be ready for the evening rush hour. With its foundries, potteries, brickworks and factories it had few pretensions to beauty, but it was home and for Miranda signified the most exciting substance in the world.

She sat in the speeding launch, remembering how as a little girl she had waited each day for her father to bring home smoothed-off scraps of glass from the factory for her to play with. She could recall staring into the depths of the lead crystal, holding up pieces to the light, and feeling that odd little catch of the heart which she still experienced whenever she saw really beautiful glass.

The fascination of it never left her, and over the years it became clear that the golden-haired child who haunted her great-uncle's glass works had been endowed with both her mother's artistic flair and her father's practical ability. It had seemed merely a natural progression when at last she began a degree course in glass at the big College of Art in a town not far from home.

Her father had been proud but slightly stunned when his eldest child, and a girl at that, revealed technical knowledge far surpassing his own at the same age. Then, when she had started making glass and came home red-cheeked and exhilarated after a day at the furnaces, her brothers would tease her, but Frank Brown just eyed his daughter with deep unease.

'Don't get set on the actual making of it, pet; at least not in industry,' he had warned. 'There's still a lot of opposition to women on the job, especially the blowing. It's no job for a woman.'

Miranda had just smiled serenely. 'Don't worry, Dad. I don't want to go into industry, at least, not full-time. I wouldn't mind being a guest designer for one of the big companies, though. That might be good, but I think I'll aim at a studio of my own, eventually.'

'Those are big ambitions, pet. I know they run a flexible course at the college these days, but I don't want them filling your head with lots of ideas that can never come to anything.'

Miranda sat in the speeding launch and smiled. Poor Dad. He'd still looked a bit baffled that morning when he saw her off at Birmingham New Street. Baffled, but proud. 'Bye, pet,' he said, holding her close. 'Take care, and remember that the Black Country can show those

Venetians a thing or two about glass-making.'

True, thought his daughter, but she had chosen a specialised branch of the craft, and one she could learn little about at home. Glass sculpture was fiendishly difficult, and it was an art in which the Venetians excelled. That was why she was sitting in this launch, zooming across a mist-wreathed stretch of water. Just then the roar of the engine faded, and she knew they must have crossed the lagoon. The mist was less dense now, and she looked out eagerly to see if Venice itself was visible. Tall buildings loomed dimly ahead, fronting the water, and she found she was holding her breath.

There, above her, she could just make out what might be an old warehouse, and then the mist swirled and parted, revealing to her horrified gaze a high brick wall topped by the unmistakable shape of a gasometer. She felt her jaw drop in dismay. Her first sight of Venice was a derelict warehouse and the gas works.

The launch edged gently along a narrow waterway, nosing between buildings whose upper floors were lost to sight. By now she had gathered her wits. In all her studying of the map of Venice she had missed the fact that the most direct route from the airport was to the mainland side of the city. She would have to wait for a sight of that celebrated waterfront.

A moment later the launch slid under a low white bridge, causing the restless mist to eddy and swirl. She emerged from the cabin and saw they were at a canal bank between two small bridges only a few yards distant from each other. The man at the wheel turned to face her, drops of moisture from his oilskins spinning through the air. He held out a large, cold hand to help her alight.

'Signorina, here is the house where you stay,' said Baldassare Gastone Antelami.

*   *   *

He delivered her into the care of her landlady, Signora Gaspari, and then touched his peaked cap in farewell. Reluctant to see him go, Miranda looked beyond him to where she could just perceive the outline of the boat. 'Thank you,' she said warmly in Italian. 'You've been very kind. I'm sorry you had such a long wait at the airport.'

His heavy features broke into a smile at hearing his own language spoken, but without more words he lifted his hand in farewell, palm foremost, rather as a priest might bestow a blessing. She knew a stab of regret as he walked away, then all was bustle as the plump, grey-haired Signora ushered her upstairs.

To Miranda the tall house seemed badly lit, full of deep shadows broken by sudden pools of light. She heard an odd assortment of music from behind closed doors—jazz, Wagner and Italian pop—and wondered if there were students staying there.

The older woman addressed her in slurred and rapid Venetian dialect, which Miranda deciphered with difficulty. When she tried out her own Italian again, the older woman concentrated with narrowed eyes, beaming in congratulation when she at last understood. On to her own bed-sitter then, lamp-lit and shuttered against the dusk. Miranda had never before lived away from home, and once alone she prowled the room, opening deep drawers and huge cupboards that smelled of pot-pourri. It was a bit of a let-down, she admitted soberly, as was Venice itself, come to that.

Suppose the job was a let-down too? Suppose the dei Santi glass works was dingy and faded and out of date? Suppose—her lower lip jutted out in disbelief—suppose she didn't come up to their expectations?

After all, she'd been invited to Venice because of a fluke. It had been sheer luck that her first decent piece of glass sculpture should have been entered for the student section of the EEC Crafts Exhibition in Paris earlier that year. Thoughtfully Miranda collected her shampoo and toilet bag, remembering for the hundredth time the January morning when Bill Wardle, Head of the Department, had sent for her.

'Miranda, your entry in the Paris Exhibition has obviously impressed a few people. We've had enquiries about your work from the French in Nancy, and a more specific one from Venice. An offer, in fact.'

She had stared at him. 'An offer? To buy it?'

He had shaken his head, smiling. 'No. You're not going to make a fortune just yet. I've had a long phone call from the firm of dei Santi, asking about our course of study here, and your work in particular.'

Miranda's great blue eyes had opened wide in amazement. 'You don't mean *Benvenuto* dei Santi? Asking about *me*? But what did you tell him?'

'Sit down, Miranda, before you fall down.' Bill Wardle had cleared a space on his cluttered table and perched on the edge of it, opposite her. 'Yes. Benvenuto dei Santi himself. He wanted to know how long you'd been doing glass sculpture, and I said you'd messed about for a while at the experimental stage, but only actually finished three or four pieces. Then he asked if you'd trained in sculpture proper—other than glass—and I told him only elementary pieces at "A" Level and maybe a bit in your own time. Oh, and that you've just started a few sessions in the sculpture workshops of the Fine Arts department here. That's right, I take it?'

'Yes, yes,' Miranda had agreed hurriedly. 'Yes. Go on.'

'Then he asked how far you'd got in the course, and I said you're on the run up to your finals; that you'd already done your thesis, and that you've only two more short papers to sit in June, and that from now on all your time will be spent in preparing your show for the external assessors.'

'And—what did he say then?'

'In a nutshell, he offered to take you on over there for six months as a gesture of goodwill from his firm to the EEC.'

'Over there?' she had echoed faintly. 'In *Venice*?'

'Yes. You'd have to come back here to put your show together and sit your theory papers, of course.'

But she had had misgivings about the piece of work that had brought about this situation. Dozens of experiments had led to her making the head of a baby, modelled on her little half-brother, Bobby. Far too ambitious for her skills, it had succeeded in a way that even Miranda didn't fully understand. She could see things in the finished head that hadn't even occurred to her when she was working on it, and thought that the glass itself encouraged light and shade to paint their own pictures on it.

Her father and stepmother had gone to see the display of students' work at the college open evening. Mr Brown had been taken aback. To him, the brilliant cut-crystal ware that was one of the glories of the Black Country was infinitely more impressive than his daughter's strange, way-out sculptures; but Betty, his wife for the last two years, had been delighted that a head of her son was being sent to a Paris exhibition.

'I do think you're clever, love,' she had said, giving Miranda one of her frequent squeezes. 'Just look at these chubby little cheeks. He was just like that at eight months. Anyone in their senses can see that it's the best thing on show.'

Miranda had doubted very much whether anyone who knew about glass would share Betty's biased opinion, but now here was this incredible offer. She had

eyed Bill Wardle obstinately. 'But—I have to admit that
the baby's head was—well, a bit of a fluke. It turned
out better than I had any right to expect.'

'So?'

'So I don't know if I'd be any good to dei Santi, if I'd
be any use to him. He shouldn't really judge me on the
baby's head, should he? And anyway, what will I have
to do over there?'

'What he tells you, I imagine,' said Bill Wardle drily.
'You'll probably be a general dogsbody at first, and
he's suggested a month's trial on either side. But don't
underestimate yourself, Miranda. You must know
you're one of our star pupils—why do you think we
were all so relieved when you decided at last what to
specialise in? From the college's point of view I must
admit I'm pretty pleased with dei Santi's offer.'

'But aren't the Venetians supposed to be highly
secretive about their methods?' she had persisted.

He'd laughed. 'You know, I suppose, that in the
sixteenth century they sent assassins after any glass-
makers who emigrated, to prevent the giving away of
trade secrets, but I think we can take it that they've
progressed a bit since then. Dei Santi's certainly have
the reputation of being progressive, and it appears that
like other top firms over there they're experimenting
with glass sculpture, and want someone with aptitude,
even if only a beginner, to both train and assist in their
glasshouse on the island of Murano. What do you say?
Shall we find out some more before you decide?'

From then on things had moved fast. In his element,
Bill Wardle had conducted the negotiations on her
behalf. In three weeks it was all settled. She would go
out to Venice from mid-April to mid-October, returning
home for two weeks in June to assemble her show and
sit her two exams. Her air fare and accommodation
would be paid for by the dei Santi firm, who would also

pay her a weekly wage equivalent to what an Italian trainee at her level would receive.

That settled, she had signed a brief agreement, and by return received a copy of the letter from Benvenuto dei Santi to the EEC and a personal letter confirming the terms of her employment. Both were signed in elegant black script: *Benvenuto Gabriele Sante dei Santi*. And a name like that, she thought in amusement, put her father's plain Frank Brown firmly into perspective.

Dei Santi—that meant 'of the Saints', didn't it? Sante dei Santi must be 'Saint of the Saints', and with Gabriele thrown in for good measure ... Her imagination had conjured up a picture of an elderly master craftsman with an austere, saintly profile and a mane of silvery hair, reminiscent of a picture she'd seen of one of the early doges. The dreamy romanticism inherited from her mother ran strong in Miranda, given half a chance.

The other side of her nature was severely practical, and then it had moved into overdrive. She had studied Italian technical terms in a manual sent from Venice, and began a crash course in the spoken language. Her small bedroom had echoed to melodious phrases from her cassettes, and her answers to the oft-repeated questions sent her brothers into fits of rude teenage laughter.

She made for the bathroom, her spirits lifting. Venice wasn't going to be all gasometers and warehouses; and as for the legendary dei Santi with his string of elegant names—well, she might like him. Even more important— he might like her!

Back in her room she was about to put on her jeans and a clean shirt when there was a knock at the door and an urgent cry from Signora Gaspari. 'Signorina! Signorina!'

Miranda rushed to open the door, and there on the landing was a tall, unsmiling man in a black leather coat, with the landlady hovering respectfully at his side.

She set up an agonised gabble when she saw Miranda's skimpy towelling robe, but the man dismissed her with a wave of the hand and strode over the threshold, closing the door behind him.

'Benvenuto dei Santi,' he said.

Hair still wet, her feet bare, devoid of make-up and wearing a mini-length bath robe, Miranda looked up at her new employer. He was dark, with thick hair that had a dull sheen to it. The face was arresting rather than handsome, without a vestige of spare flesh over the high-boned cheeks and aggressive jaw line. The light from above cast deep shadows under his brows, but she could see that the watchful eyes were grey, clear as river water. He's young, she thought, amazed; in his early thirties . . . Her nebulous mental pictures vanished. This was no silver-haired saint, no father-figure, and she felt her heart thud, just once.

For some seconds the man said no more, but looked at her with a touch of the same surprise as that shown by the boatman at the airport. Miranda looked back at him uneasily. Evidently she wasn't what they'd expected. At last he put out his hand and said, 'I've come to see that all's well with you. I hear you had a delayed journey.'

What English! Excellent, and with of all things, an American accent. He sounded human after all, in spite of his glittering reputation and the cool, calculating stare. Relieved, Miranda beamed up at him and gave him her own small hand, warm and still a trifle damp. 'Yes, we were two hours late, but everything's all right, thanks. It's kind of you to come round in person . . . er . . . won't you sit down?'

She wiggled her fingers but he kept hold of her hand, and to her astonishment turned it back and forth, scrutinising it with interest. 'It's a very small hand,' he said. 'Glass-making is heavy work, Miranda Brown.'

'Yes,' she agreed, 'I do know that. But I manage.'

The Venetian deposited the inadequate hand firmly against her middle, then went and sat in one of the room's two comfortable chairs. Miranda perched on the edge of the other one, tugging furtively at the hem of her robe. She'd shown more leg dozens of times, but not in a dimly-lit room with a high bed close by, and confronted by a stranger.

Male-female relationships seemed far from dei Santi's mind, however. He watched her thoughtfully, then said, 'Don't disturb yourself, I'm leaving in just a moment. This place,' he waved a hand and looked round the room doubtfully, 'do you think it will do?'

'Oh, yes. I'm sure it will be splendid,' she said hastily. After all, he was paying for it.

He nodded. 'Good. And Venice—you've seen little of her so far?'

Something in the way he said it, a touch of doting pride; and the way he almost, but not quite, managed to summon a smile, made Miranda reply rashly, 'I've seen nothing at all so far, apart from the mist, a derelict warehouse, and the gas works.'

It sounded an ungracious statement from one who had been courteously looked after since the moment she arrived, but dei Santi just moved one well-shod foot up and down, then pursed his lips thoughtfully. Then he said, 'The mist is a constant hazard here, especially at the changing of the seasons. The derelict warehouse you refer to was probably a dwelling house—you'll find before long that the exterior of Venetian houses often belies what's inside them, and'—he shook his head reprovingly—'I'm afraid that even Venice needs a gas works. You must agree that it's tucked away very discreetly. Still—you were disappointed?'

'Just a bit,' she admitted, attempting a smile. She was tired, her head ached and she was ravenously hungry. 'I realise I was silly, but I've read so much about Venice, and I was longing to see the Doges Palace and the Grand Canal—and—everything.' Her voice trailed away as it dawned on her that she sounded ridiculously sorry for herself.

The cool grey gaze remained on her flushed face, black lashes fringing his half lowered lids. 'Then this is your first visit?'

'Yes,' she said simply. There was no need to tell him that apart from a family holiday in Brittany it was her first visit anywhere abroad.

He drummed long fingers on the arm of his chair. 'It's our custom when travelling around the city to take the shortest route between two points, rather than the most beautiful,' he said gently. 'Baldassare would do just that today, but you would have seen little, whatever your route. Still, the mist will lift now the tide has changed, and you have the weekend ahead of you for sightseeing.' He stood up suddenly. 'Have you brought wellingtons?'

Miranda's eyes widened. 'Wellingtons? Wellington *boots*? No. Why?'

He sighed audibly. 'As you've read so much about Venice I should have thought you'd know that it's the time of the *acque alte*—the high waters. We haven't finished with the spring tides, and several parts of the city are flooded daily. The only sensible way to get about on foot is to wear wellingtons.'

Miranda couldn't help glancing at his own footwear, expensive leather slip-ons. 'To get about on foot,' he repeated. 'I'm travelling by boat, but in any case the tide is on the ebb now. I'll be in touch about Monday.'

'Thank you,' she said quietly.

He hesitated, and she thought he looked as if he didn't know how to phrase what he wanted to say next. But she was wrong, apparently, because he looked her up and down and said, 'I expect you could do with an early night. You must have had a tiring day.'

With that deflating remark he turned to go, but at the door whirled round to face her and smiled with sudden, heart-shaking charm. 'Oh—I almost forgot. Welcome to Venice, Miranda Brown.'

She fell asleep to the mournful hoot of ships' fog-horns, and was wakened early by the eerie rise and fall of a siren, loud enough to be heard all over Venice.

Unlatching the heavy shutters she gazed out on a cloudless blue sky, and looking down saw an old lady crossing the small paved square which she knew was called a *campo*. Three sides of the square were lined with houses in cream, pink and russet, and on the fourth side two little bridges spanned a narrow canal whose opaque green waters were sparked with gold from the sun. The scene was so totally un-English that she found herself smiling broadly from pleasure and excitement.

She turned to her other window, realising it must overlook the canal. Sure enough, when she leaned out she could see water lapping against the walls of the house, with waves from a passing boat sucking at the ancient stonework. She slipped into her robe and made for the bathroom. Ahead of her lay a whole weekend in which to explore Venice.

As she came down to the first floor the Signora emerged from her kitchen, all eyes and teeth and chatter, ready to show Miranda the system of self-service used at the breakfast table, and to introduce the solitary occupant of the dining room.

'Monsieur Antoine Bonsart!' she intoned, as if announcing a guest at a state banquet. 'French!' she added triumphantly. 'Also, I have the Belgian, the Greek, two Hollanders, the German, and one other young lady, also French. That is in addition to my two young men from Verona. They all come to Venice, to this house. It is remarkable, is it not?'

'Quite remarkable,' agreed Miranda, somewhat daunted. She hadn't bargained on such an international gathering. She helped herself to juice, coffee, and a couple of rolls with soft white cheese, while a further torrent of information revealed that such a mixture of nationalities was due to a Council of Europe school for craftsmen being, literally, just around the corner.

At last, Miranda and the young Frenchman were left alone to make small talk. He was a serious type, with kind brown eyes behind heavy spectacles, and he seemed surprised that Miranda was 'entering industry' as he put it. He was just offering to escort her round the sights of Venice, and she was trying to frame a tactful refusal, when the Signora burst upon them once more.

'Signorina! The telephone. Hurry, it is the Maestro!'

Miranda almost choked over her last mouthful. The Maestro? That could only mean Benvenuto dei Santi. Honestly! She went to the telephone at the head of the stairs. 'Hello? Miranda Brown here.'

'Dei Santi,' came the deep confident tones. 'I trust you're rested?'

'Oh yes, thank you.'

'Good. I've arranged for you to travel down the Grand Canal this morning. Baldassare will pick you up in half an hour.'

Her cherished mental vision of exploring the city alone began to evaporate. 'But—but I thought I'd go— er—well—that is——'

He cut in briskly. 'We must make up for yesterday's disappointment, mustn't we? You heard the siren?'

'Yes, I did. What was it for?'

'A warning that the high water is here again—the flooding. We hear it almost daily at certain times of the year. Have you not noticed the little waterway at Due Ponti?'

That was the name of the *campo* outside. Due Ponti—Two Bridges. 'I've seen the canal here, yes. It does look a bit full to overflowing,' she admitted.

'Of course. It happens often, you know—too often. You must see about wellingtons later this morning. Be ready in half an hour.'

Miranda glared at the unoffending wall paper behind the telephone. 'Yes, Mr dei Santi,' she said sweetly, and replaced the receiver with exaggerated care.

CHAPTER TWO

MIRANDA eyed her reflection dubiously. A trip down the Grand Canal seemed to call for clothes other than her serviceable jeans and checked shirt. She substituted her best pale blue trousers and a pink shirt with a frilled collar, changed her training shoes for flat leather pumps, and put on her blue angora sweater beneath the inevitable cord jacket. That was a bit better. She didn't want Baldassare to feel let down by his passenger.

She went down to wait for him by the ornamental well-head in the middle of the *campo*; the black iron cover was ice-cold when she touched it, and she was glad she'd thought to wear the sweater. On time to the minute, Baldassare Antelami stopped the launch between the two bridges and she went towards him, beaming as if at an old friend. 'Good morning, Signor.'

He returned her greeting courteously, then helped her aboard and she stood at his side as they slid away from the *campo*. 'You do well with our language, Signorina,' he said gently.

Her spirits soared. He could understand her accent, and he was nice; the sun was shining and in a few minutes she would see the Grand Canal. She looked behind her at the Gaspari house, painted deep pink with green shutters. She could see now that it had a roof garden, where plants in new spring growth tumbled over wooden railings. It was right over her bedroom too—she had a garden above her as she slept! All at once she felt ridiculously flattered and comforted, as if someone had arranged a special surprise for her.

They sailed on under more bridges, past buildings in

muted pinks and fawns then turned sharply, heading
for open water, and a moment later Miranda gasped in
pleasure. They were out in the lagoon, where a strong
wind was smacking little white crested waves into each
other, making them dance and sparkle in the sun.

Away across the water was low-lying land toppled by
close-packed buildings and a white lighthouse. 'That is
Murano,' said her companion, and for the first time she
looked on the small island which was to be her work
place. At that moment she would willingly have
relinquished her escorted trip in favour of a good look
round the dei Santi works and a clear idea of what she
would be expected to do once she was inside.

Then they were picking up speed across the choppy
water, the boatman controlling the wheel with casual
flicks of a wrist, his other arm resting against the brass
rail at his side. To her left was a long quayside, where
water was already overlapping the stone edging.

Before long Baldassare turned back into the shelter of
the city canals, slowing to the orderly crawl that seemed
to be obligatory there. Moments later they stopped at a
landing stage and tied up next to the elegant black
shape of a gondola. It swayed there at its mooring,
immaculate paintwork edged with gold, its cushions
padded with blue silk, and a winged lion, symbol of
Venice, embossed on its prow.

'Signorina,' said the boatman, holding out his hand.
Puzzled, she allowed herself to be helped ashore, to
stand on boards laid along the quayside. She couldn't
understand why they'd stopped, she knew this wasn't
the Grand Canal. Inevitably her gaze went back to the
gondola. It was the first she'd seen, apart from pictures
and photographs, and almost without realising she was
doing it she leaned forward and touched the black body
with gentle fingertips.

'Good morning,' said Benvenuto dei Santi behind her.

She shot upright. 'Oh!' The syllable came out, unflatteringly, as a wail. She hadn't expected to see him. The bright pink of her cheeks deepened, and she ran cold fingers over her wind-tossed hair. 'Oh—good morning,' she amended hurriedly, striving to sound pleased.

In broad daylight her employer looked more cool and self-possessed than ever. He was wearing a roll-necked white sweater under a jacket of heavy grey suede, and his trousers were tucked into wellingtons.

She saw at once that he hadn't missed the tone of her first, involuntary greeting. A touch of colour ran beneath the high cheekbones, and his upper lip was lifted slightly, revealing white teeth clamped irritably together. The eyes seemed darker than she remembered, and now they were watching her narrowly. 'You're surprised to see me?' he asked edgily.

'Yes,' she admitted.

'But why? I'm taking you down the Grand Canal. Did you not realise it? Baldassare—a rug for the Signorina.'

Without more ado he stepped into the gondola and held out a hand to help her follow him. Miranda hesitated, wondering if he was bossy simply because he was Venetian. She'd read that they were an extremely proud and high-handed people, and that many of them still refused to consider themselves part of the Italian nation. It began to dawn on her that it might be no picnic working for such a man.

A curly-haired gondolier moved forward, wearing the traditional short black jacket and striped jersey, and took his stance ready to cast off. Benvenuto dei Santi saw her comfortably seated, placed the rug across her knees, and then sat down next to her in the high-backed double seat. With a flick of his fingers he signalled to the gondolier to move off.

Miranda, tucked under a rug for the second time in two days, looked sideways at her employer's profile and began to feel distinctly uncomfortable. It had been plain that he knew she'd been dismayed to see him, yet here he was, concealing justifiable annoyance, apparently as willing to proceed as if she'd fallen all over him in welcome.

When she turned her head she could see the easy, unhurried stroke of the gondolier as he stood behind them, plying his single oar. Biting her lip, she decided that nothing must be allowed to spoil the coming moments. She cudgelled her wits for a way of making amends for her rudeness, and at last brought forth two sentences in her best Italian.

'This is really most kind of you, Signor. I deeply appreciate the fact that you are taking the trouble to accompany me in person.'

His face was only inches away, his eyes fixed on her in the intent, analytical regard she remembered only too well from the previous evening, as if they would very soon decipher whatever chaotic thoughts were whirling through her mind. At such close quarters she could see that the clear grey irises were flecked with blue, and that his skin was fine-textured and smooth, except around the shadowed jaw-line.

But if Miranda was taking the opportunity for a closer look at him, he was doing the same with her, and seemed in no hurry to finish his scrutiny. She moistened her lips uneasily. Why didn't he answer? Did he think her Italian so awful it defied comment?

He shook his head, as if dismissing an idea or impression, and bestowed on her the second smile of their brief acquaintance. At such close range it was overpoweringly attractive, and the mad thought flashed into her mind that it had the same effect on her as the white-hot light of a glass-furnace. She took a deep breath and forced herself to look elsewhere.

'Your accent is good,' was his eventual prosaic comment. 'Well done. But relax now and keep to English. Later on you'll find plenty of opportunity to practise your Italian.' Then he went on with no change of tone, 'I can quite understand that you want to be alone to explore Venice, and I promise that in an hour or so I'll leave you free to do just that. Last night, though, I had the idea that a journey by gondola would appeal to you.'

'But it does,' she agreed quickly. 'It appeals very much.'

He made no reply to that, and they sailed on towards a wider expanse of water, where in a single leisurely curve they swung out into the Grand Canal. Sunlight slanted towards them from a clear sky, throwing the ancient buildings into colourful relief above the restless green water.

'Oh——' she breathed faintly.

Behind them the gondolier began to recite the names of the palaces and noble houses on either side. '*Ca' d'Oro*,' he called.

Benvenuto dei Santi leaned back in the seat, watching her reactions. 'We are some distance down the canal already, as you may know. I asked Baldassare to bring you to this point because from here onwards you will see the most impressive stretch.' After a moment he said musingly, 'Miranda . . . a beautiful name . . . Prospero's daughter . . . Does it signify that your parents are devotees of Shakespeare?'

'Yes. At least, my mother was. She died in an accident when I was seventeen.'

The observant eyes flickered and remained steadily on hers. 'My condolences,' he said quietly, 'and my regrets at having brought it to your mind on what I hoped would be a happy occasion for you.'

'Don't have regrets,' she protested. 'I'm always

thinking of her. She was—very dear to me.' When he didn't reply she rushed on, as if compelled to fill the silence, 'My two brothers are named after Shakespearean characters as well. They're called Sebastian and Benedick, but they prefer Seb and Dick.'

'The baby?' he asked, puzzled. 'One of them is the baby—your head of the child in glass? I was told that it was your brother, but I was doubtful about the age difference . . .'

'Oh no. The baby's head was taken from Bobby, my little half-brother. My father has married again, you see.' Her voice trailed away. The gondola had rounded a curve in the Canal and ahead of them lay, unmistakably, the Rialto Bridge.

At once Miranda was taken back in time to her little room at home, studying for her English 'O' Levels. Her mother had been marvellous at helping with her homework, and one of that year's set books had been *The Merchant of Venice*. In Shakespeare's day the area of the Rialto had housed the money-lenders and merchants of the city, and perhaps did so still . . .

Unaware that the man at her side was watching her closely, she stared wide-eyed as they approached the bridge. Memories that she'd thought were stored tidily away came tumbling urgently to light. How her mother would have loved to see all this!

Suddenly, to her deep embarrassment, Miranda felt tears start to her eyes and hang trembling on her lashes. Her heart lurched in protest—it was ages since she'd wept for her mother. She couldn't prevent the tears from rolling down her cheeks, so she turned her head away and faced the opposite bank, blinking rapidly. If he saw her crying he would think she was morbid, or neurotic, or both.

'Miranda.'

Reluctantly she faced him, her huge eyes brimming.

'This is distressing you,' he said tightly. And then, proof that he understood exactly what had upset her, he added, 'There's still to come the house where Othello is said to have lived with his Desdemona.'

Miranda mopped her eyes. This outing was proving to be a disaster, and she could blame nobody but herself. 'I shouldn't cry,' she said simply, 'because all my memories of her are happy ones.'

And all at once it seemed quite fitting that he should pat her hand consolingly, quite natural that they should continue their progress along that celebrated waterway, and absolutely right that the gondolier should still call out his sing-song recital of the palaces on either side.

Miranda sat on the low parapet of a bridge eating a banana and drinking milk from a carton. She felt as tired as if she'd just finished a hot day in front of the furnaces, though in reality she'd exerted herself very little. It was the strangeness of everything, she told herself, and in particular it was the stress of dealing with her new boss, or to be more exact, getting used to the way he dealt with her.

Cringing mentally, she looked back on her over-wrought behaviour in the gondola. If anybody had told her before she left England that Benvenuto dei Santi would take her down the Grand Canal on her first day in Venice she would have laughed in their face; and if they'd told her that on the same outing she would cry for her mother she would have dismissed the idea as madness.

But that was what had happened, and she had to admit that her employer had come out of the episode with some credit. After that first hint of anger he'd accepted her distress with a sort of down-to-earth compassion and their journey had somehow regained its magic. Instead of feeling awkward she became more at

ease, and able to absorb the unique loveliness of Venice,
sitting there silent and quite spellbound.

As they neared St Mark's he pointed to the tall
windows of a showroom fronting the Canal. 'That's
where I live,' he said casually, 'in winter, at any rate.'

Miranda stared. 'You live on the Grand Canal?
But—are those your showrooms?'

He seemed amused. 'Who else's? As you say in
England, I "live over the shop". You must have a look
round there in a few days' time when you're settled in.
We have some interesting old pieces on permanent
display.'

Visions came to her of dozens of dei Santis occupying
the huge building. 'Your family?' she asked hesitantly.
'You all live there?'

'No. You may come across other dei Santis in
Venice, but I'm the last of our particular line, and I live
there alone now. My father lives in Verona because of
his health, and so do my two sisters and their families.'

She digested that in silence. No Signora dei Santi
then, and no little dei Santis ... She'd thought all
Italians were pressurised into matrimony by their
families ... And the father he spoke of must be the
great Alessandro dei Santi ... At least she wouldn't
have him to contend with when she started work on
Murano ...

Soon the gondolier was edging his craft into place at
the very waterfront that had occupied her daydreams
for so long. She was amazed at the sight of waves
rolling gently, inexorably, beneath the exquisite arcades
of the Doges Palace and up to the entrance of the
Basilica itself. Lines of people trooped patiently along
the boardwalks above the flood water, while in the
Piazza a few lighthearted souls waded around knee
deep, cameras at the ready. She was torn between
excitement at the scene and bewilderment at how to

cope. It was obviously time to say 'thanks and goodbye'
to dei Santi, so should she gaily step ashore and wade
to the boards, or what?

Her companion didn't leave her in doubt for long. He
took her firmly by the arm and helped her to her feet;
then, keeping his balance with no apparent effort,
picked her up in his arms, stepped from the gondola,
and waded through the water as calmly as if she were a
toddler and he a proud papa.

It seemed to Miranda that there must be hundreds,
thousands, *millions* of people watching, and her cheeks
flamed as they were pressed close to his chest. She
longed to wriggle free, but was frightened of landing on
her bottom in the water. He marched to the nearest
boards and set her down lightly, one arm steadying her;
then without any sign of either irritation or pleasure at
having had to carry her in full view of what seemed to
be half the population of Venice, he stepped up beside
her and said, 'Right, let's go and get you some
wellingtons.'

Still on the board walk, she followed him across the
Piazza, giving the incredible façade of St Mark's no
more than an astounded stare in passing; then on
beneath an ancient clock tower into a narrow crowded
thoroughfare. 'This is the main shopping street,' said
dei Santi over his shoulder, 'the Merceria. We'll soon be
beyond the water.'

They descended to street level, where he took her arm
and threaded his way through the crowds. Miranda
glimpsed small, luxurious shops, but there was no time
to linger, because he marched her into one of them—a
shoe shop. 'Dei Santi,' he said.

The saleslady, obviously pre-warned, proceeded to
measure Miranda's feet with as much care as if she was
aiming to sell a pair of the exquisite shoes in the
window, while dei Santi watched with interest. Miranda

began to see that he was a man who was interested in everything. There was nothing about him of the creative genius in his own little world, his eyes on the stars; he had his eyes fixed all too observantly on what went on in the world around him.

Stylish blue wellies chosen, he waved her purse aside and sailed out of the shop with a slightly dazed Miranda trotting after him.

Back in the street he handed her a map of the city. 'You'll find this useful,' he said. 'It shows the *vaporetto* routes and numbers, and the times they sail; being public transport they're pretty frequent. You can go and explore now to your heart's content ... alone.' She looked at him closely when he said that, but could detect no touch of humour, or resentment either. He knew quite well that she'd wanted to be on her own, and merely mentioned it as a fact.

'One last point,' he said. 'Glass. You'll see hundreds of glass shops in Venice. Some sell rubbish, others middle of the road stuff and a few, perhaps no more than ten or twelve, sell top-quality Venetian glass. Look at those few shops, Miranda, and try to ignore the rest.' He looked down at her. 'Off you go and enjoy yourself.'

Now that the moment had come she found she wasn't at all sure that she wanted to be on her own, after all; but he was obviously ready to leave her. Perhaps he considered that he'd done his duty to his English student. 'Thank you,' she said earnestly, 'for everything.'

He nodded, gave a hint of the smile, took her hand for an instant and bent his head politely, then turned on his heel and headed back to the Piazza. At once she rushed after him and grabbed his arm. 'Mr dei Santi! What about Monday? Where's the works? How do I get there and what time do I start?'

They stood face to face among the press of the

crowd, she agitated, he shaking his head reprovingly. 'Don't excite yourself—I would have contacted you before then. Be at the *vaporetto* landing stage on the Fondamente Nuove—the one nearest your *pensione*. The stage itself is called 'Celestia'. I'll pick you up there at eight.'

'Oh!' Her eyes widened. Surely he didn't intend her to sail to Murano with him every day? 'Thanks,' she added hurriedly.

But the careful eyes were watching her. 'Just for the first few days,' he said a trifle wearily. 'After that Baldassare can take you or you can use public transport. You must travel however you wish. Until Monday, then.'

He turned and walked away without a backward glance, while Miranda stood watching him. Was it her imagination or did he seem reluctant to go into any detail about her work at his firm? There, among the morning crowds on the Merceria, she felt a chilly breath of doubt. Perhaps he was already having second thoughts about inviting an unknown beginner to work in his studio? If so, why had he spent time with her that morning—been so surprisingly obliging . . .?

She turned in the opposite direction and gave a little shrug. Monday morning would come soon enough, and then she would know exactly what was facing her. She walked purposefully ahead. If this was the main shopping street of Venice she should soon come across one of the few good glass shops.

In the Piazza arcades she found some of the good glass shops and was stunned by what was on sale. She had examined the sculptures minutely; dazzling abstracts from Seguso, figures from life by Rosin; world-famous names and some that were new to her. The technique took her breath away, and when she thought of her own work—the baby's head—she didn't know whether to be glad or sorry that she was in a city where such work was produced as a matter of course.

She saw nothing at all under the name dei Santi, and wondered why. Was it that he sold his wares only from the elegant showrooms on the other side of the Grand Canal?

She studied her map, deciding where to make for next. Tomorrow she must check on the whereabouts of the *vaporetto* stage where she was to be picked up on Monday. He'd said its name was 'Celestia'.

All at once she found herself chuckling. 'Celestia'—it was certainly a change from the bus stop on Walsall Road.

CHAPTER THREE

On Monday morning Miranda left the Campo Due Ponti by the bridge leading to the lagoon, and paused with her hand on the white parapet. It was sheer fancy, but it seemed just then that the little bridge symbolised the change in her life: the crossing over from her long studentship into paid employment.

She made her way through the clean-swept squares and alleys while high above her, between tall houses, women were hanging out their washing. Sheets, tablecloths, shirts and petticoats flapped and billowed in the breeze from the lagoon, as neighbours called to each other from upper-floor windows. Then on beneath the crenellated walls of the Arsenal, once the mightiest shipyard in the world. She knew that those same mellow bricks had seen new galleys leave for Byzantium, and now they looked down on men stacking crates of Coca-Cola on barges to chug fussily through the city canals. Such contrasts fascinated her, but she hurried on. It was ten minutes to eight.

A sleek, dark blue launch swirled up to the quay soon after she arrived. Benvenuto dei Santi was at the controls, and all in a moment she noticed several things; the gold dei Santi crest on the cabin; a *vaporetto* clanking against the Celestia landing stage to pick up passengers for Murano; the water level that by now almost overlapped the quay, and finally her employer's face, lean and intent, but lit by his rare smile when he saw her waiting.

'Good morning, Miranda.' He steadied her with a firm grip as the launch rocked wildly in the swell of the *vaporetto*. 'How was your weekend?'

33

'Oh, lovely, thanks.' She sounded breathless, and no wonder, she thought, with all this stepping on and off wildly rocking boats. He opened the cabin but she said, 'No. I'll stay out here if I may. I can see more.'

She put down her folio of drawings and a bag containing her shoes and working dungarees, and saw that dei Santi was wearing a black leather jacket with, presumably, working clothes underneath. He might head the company but she knew he also worked at his craft.

He swung the launch out into the lagoon, where they picked up speed and headed towards the little island that lay between them and Murano. Miranda eyed it eagerly. White-banded walls of deep red brick rose straight from the water, topped by dark cypresses which swayed beneath the pale sky.

'This is the cemetery island ahead, isn't it?' she asked as the high red walls loomed nearer.

He looked down at her, slightly amused. 'That's right, San Michele. It's strange how it fascinates the English and the Americans. My relations from the States always have it high on their lists of "sights not to be missed".'

She turned to look up at him. 'You have relations in the States, Mr dei Santi?'

'Lots of them,' he admitted. 'Mostly cousins and half cousins. My mother was American.'

She might have guessed. His accent for one thing, and for another his appearance. True, he was dark-haired, but his skin wasn't swarthy, and she had thought the set of his features quite un-Italian, not to mention those eyes ... If it came to that, his manner and the way he conducted himself seemed un-Italian too ...

They zoomed on past the tranquil cemetery island. 'It's not misty this morning,' he stated mildly.

'No,' agreed Miranda. Surely he wasn't one to remark on the obvious?

'And so you've had no difficulty in seeing the mountains?'

'Mountains?' she repeated. 'What mountains?'

He chuckled, a deep throaty sound full of amusement. 'Well, even in the mist you spotted the gas-works, so naturally I didn't think you'd miss the Alps. There they are, Miranda Brown. The Alps—to the north.' He pointed ahead, slightly to her left.

There, so far distant they seemed like a dream-image, soared the snow-capped peaks of the Alps, high and remote and unbelievably beautiful. The tension that had bedevilled her since she awoke vanished in an upsurge of joy. She stood on tip-toe and said the first thing that came into her head. 'Oh, thank you. Thank you for telling me! I might have missed them. I had no idea they'd be visible from Venice!'

She beamed up at him and surprised a strange expression on his face, at once uncomfortable and rather sad; almost—but surely not—almost guilty. He acknowledged her impulsive outburst with a mere nod, and said shortly, 'They aren't always visible. Today the air is clear and the wind is right.' Then he fell silent. Constraint came between them, but her spirits were still soaring. The sight of the far-off mountains had raised her morale, just like the time she'd first seen the roof garden over her room at the Gaspari house. She kept quiet while they followed the shore line of Murano, to slacken speed at last and dip to a halt at a stone landing stage. There was nothing to be seen except a high wall with an arched gateway, and behind them the empty water stretching away to the mainland.

Dei Santi leapt ashore and tied up. He helped her alight and glanced down just once at her blue wellingtons. She wondered if, like her, he was remembering how he'd carried her ashore from the gondola; but his brisk, businesslike tones soon dispelled that idea.

'This is the water-gate of the works,' he said, 'used only for freight and for those visitors who come by special arrangement. Most of the workers use the factory entrance from the town. Allow me——' He took her packages and led her to the archway with its iron-banded gates.

'It looks awfully old,' she ventured.

He pointed to a date carved in the stonework: *1500.* 'It is awfully old,' he agreed gravely, his gaze lingering on the weather-worn numerals. Then he turned to her, one hand grasping a great bronze ring, ready to open the gate. 'I've kept part of the morning free in order to show you round and see you settled in. But first I think we should have a talk.'

'So do I,' agreed Miranda promptly. The sure instinct which sometimes swept aside all commonsense and reason told her that something about employing her made him uneasy. Still, if they were to have a talk presumably she would find out what it was?

Once through the gate she could hear a sound she knew well; the dull, continuous roar of furnaces. She almost sighed in relief. That, at least, was familiar. They were on an arcaded walk-way which lined the walls of an enclosed yard, in the centre of which was a big, circular building that she knew must house the furnaces.

Eyes huge with interest, cheeks pink from the crossing, she smoothed her wind-tossed hair and looked eagerly around her. She'd arrived at last. Here she was in the dei Santi works. Her breathing quickened with excitement and anticipation.

The man at her side was watching her reactions closely. 'This is the original glasshouse, built by my

family almost five centuries ago when they left Venice
for Murano. The square bell tower you see over there
was built as both a landmark in the growing town and a
lookout post to watch for enemies crossing the lagoon
from the sea.'

Miranda's ready imagination at once summoned up
such a scene, while he went on, 'We've modernised
continually over the years, and built a whole new range
of buildings alongside, but this yard is still the heart of
the dei Santi enterprise. By great good fortune nobody
has tried to alter it. I want it to stay unspoiled—and so
it will—as long as I'm in charge.' She looked at the set
of that determined chin, and believed him.

'This way.' He led off at his usual pace, but just then
a young man hurried towards them and stopped in
front of dei Santi. He bobbed his head respectfully and
said, '*Buon giorno*, Maestro.'

Miranda almost groaned. That word again!
Maestro—Master. To her independent English spirit it
seemed far too subservient.

De Santi seemed to find nothing unusual in the title.
'*Buon giorno*, Innocenzo. Miranda, allow me to
introduce Innocenzo Paulucci, a most valued employee
of the company, and my technical assistant.' Then, in
Italian, 'I have the honour to present Miranda Brown,
third year student for the Bachelor of Arts degree in the
design and manufacture of glass in the renowned lead
crystal area of the English Midlands. The signorina has
recently had her work shown in the Paris Exhibition,
and as you know has joined us for a short period of
time under the auspices of the EEC.'

Dumbfounded by the high-flown introduction,
Miranda saw at once that it was only what the other
man expected. At the same time she wondered how on
earth she could have thought Benvenuto dei Santi to be
un-Italian. The moment she heard him speak his own

melodious, many-syllabled language it was as if the calm, English-American accents had never passed his lips. She felt unpleasantly bereft, as if her one link with England had been severed.

Innocenzo Paulucci had taken her hand. Confident dark eyes with extravagantly long lashes looked her up and down and up again, then he pressed his lips to her fingers. Something about the way he did it told her that he expected her to be bowled over—the little English miss swept off her feet by the handsome Italian.

She had never bothered to fulfil the expectations of confident, predatory men, and saw no reason to start now. 'How do you do?' she said with deliberate restraint, and saw irritation cloud the perfect features. Innocenzo was an unsuitable name if ever she'd heard one, she decided. There was no innocence whatsoever in those worldly-wise black eyes.

Dei Santi's cool regard was on them both, and a hint of amusement showed around his mouth. 'Is everything under control on the shop floor?' he asked the younger man.

'Yes, Maestro. All is well.'

'Good. Then try not to disturb me for a couple of hours, will you? And be so good as to tell Enrico and Armani also. The signorina and I have much to discuss.'

'As you wish.' Innocenzo lowered his eyes deferentially, and inclined his head to Miranda. 'Signorina,' he murmured politely, then walked away across the yard.

The sun was shining, the high wall behind her gave protection from the wind, and yet Miranda shivered, suddenly cold. She watched Innocenzo's rear view uneasily. Slender, of middle height, dressed in tight black jeans and a stylish striped shirt, he was just a stunningly handsome young man with a good opinion

of himself. There was nothing about him to convey a
sense of foreboding ... Her nerves must be at full
stretch.

She followed her employer into a suite of offices
where staff were just arriving. There was no woman to
be seen until he led her into a square office furnished
with restrained modern elegance. 'My office,' he said,
then opening an adjoining door, 'and my secretary's.
Ah, *buon giorno*, Felicetta.'

A small, grey-haired woman turned round from a
filing cabinet. 'Maestro!' she exclaimed, unfeignedly
glad to see him. Once more Benvenuto went through
the elaborate ritual of introductions, then asked, 'Is
there anything urgent in the mail? If not I'll go through
it later. Any messages?'

Felicetta Balbi's efficient manner softened visibly.
'Signorina Elena has already telephoned. Apparently
you suggested a birthday lunch at the Danieli?' Her
tone didn't lose its respect, but Miranda detected a hint
of reproof. A midday appointment, and his secretary
not informed?

De Santi merely raised his eyebrows and muttered
something under his breath. 'Give me a few minutes,
then get her on the phone for me, if you please. And
will you kindly order coffee for us in about half an
hour? Miranda—this way.'

Once more she followed him, this time up a flight of
stairs. He waved a hand at a doorway on the first
landing. 'My studio,' he said, but went on climbing.
'We're now in the square tower that I pointed out when
we arrived.' Then opening a door almost at the top of
the stairs, he looked at her over his shoulder. 'This
room is yours for as long as you're with us, Miranda.'

A room of her own? In the cream-coloured tower
with the pointed roof? She looked at him uncertainly,
but he was waiting for her to precede him.

It was a working studio, spacious and well equipped; with benches, cupboards, modelling and drawing equipment, easy chairs, and a small washroom partitioned off in one corner. What held Miranda's attention, though, was that in each of the four walls was a window, with shutters thrown wide to reveal glorious views.

She turned slowly, full circle, seeing in turn the distant causeway linking Venice to the mainland; the city itself with its domes and belltowers; the lagoon stretching away to the sea, and the dark Euganean hills backed by the splendour of the Alps.

It was so much more than she'd ever expected, so different from her cubby-hole corner at the college, that she felt suddenly wary. Why such a room for a mere trainee? 'It's a lovely room,' she said at last, with strain in her voice.

Still by the door, dei Santi shrugged his shoulders and raised an arm, palm uppermost, in a graceful gesture that was entirely foreign, as if acknowledging the most fulsome compliment instead of four stilted words. 'I thought you might like it,' he said simply.

'But——' It was no use, she had to say it. 'Isn't it a bit—a bit grand—for a student?'

'Mm? I don't think so. We had it renovated some years ago when we hired a Swedish designer for a new range of light fittings we were putting out. He had the reputation of being a very temperamental man, for a Swede, so we thought we'd give a him a room of his own with interesting views, to keep him happy.'

'And did it?'

'No. I'm afraid he quarrelled with my father and went back to Stockholm in a rage. Since then we've employed either our own designers or used free-lance Venetians, and the room's been used only by me when I need extra space or perhaps a little peace and quiet.'

'Oh,' she said.

He put her things down on a chair and looked at the bulging folio. 'Have you brought some of your designs?'

'No! That is—yes. Well, actually—no. Not designs, just sketches that I've done in the last few weeks.'

'Relax, relax. You're tense as strung wire. Settle yourself in and come down to my studio in five minutes. Then I'll tell you anything you want to know.' He picked up the folio again. 'I'll take this with me.'

Once he'd gone, she took out her well-thumbed dictionary and leafed through the pages. Had she translated correctly what he'd said to Innocenzo and Felicetta about her being here 'for a short space of time'? Yes, she'd been right. Surely six months couldn't be described as that? Had he already decided that the four-week trial period would be ample? She hung up her jacket and attacked her unruly hair, her mind still on his choice of phrase. Perhaps compared with five centuries of glassmaking a six-months' visit *was* a short space of time?

'Come in and sit down,' said Benvenuto dei Santi when she tapped at his open door. He was by the window above the courtyard, holding some of her drawings, and in cords and an open-necked shirt looked ready for a hard day's work. He pulled forward an easy chair, but as she sat down the phone rang. 'No—don't go,' he ordered, 'this will only take a moment.'

He picked up the phone on his work-bench. '*Pronto*? Elena? Ben. A happy birthday, pretty one. No, of course I hadn't forgotten we'd thought of lunch, but I hadn't confirmed it, either, had I? A million apologies, but I can't manage it today. I shall be too busy. I have the team standing by for one o'clock.' He listened while the voice at the other end of the line went on at length, and Miranda looked through the window as though occupied with the scene outside. It was quite a novelty to hear him laughing so indulgently.

'Elena, listen. How about drinks early this evening before we go to the theatre, and then a late meal afterwards? You'd like that? Excellent. I'll pick you up about six-thirty? He laughed again. 'Oh no! *Arrivederci*, Elena.'

'A friend of mine,' he said unnecessarily as he hung up. Sitting facing her he became serious again, and said quietly, 'Let's go through every aspect of your stay here, so that there are no unexplained factors to worry you. First, I saw that you were somewhat staggered at the name "Maestro"?'

He smiled faintly at her amazed silence. 'Your eyes are easy to read,' he said, as if that explained everything. 'Maestro means "teacher" as much as "master", you know. Here it's a sort of courtesy title for an artist in glass the same as, say, the conductor of an orchestra. You'll be familiar with the orchestration of glass-making—the way everyone plays his part in creating a harmonious piece of work?'

Miranda nodded, still as silent as if she'd been struck dumb.

'And I think that in England you would speak of a "master-craftsman"? Well, here it's the same sort of thing only we use the title face-to-face. Maestro merely denotes that a man is a master of his craft.' There was nothing immodest about the way he said it. He was stating a fact, just as if he'd said, 'This room is large and square'. He was a master of his craft. That was that.

'I see,' she said, slightly repelled by such blatant confidence. 'So I'm to address you as Maestro, then?'

'If you can manage it. Especially in the works. I know it will be yet another thing that's strange and a bit trying for you, so when there's nobody within earshot, please use my Christian name. My family and friends call me Ben.'

She repressed a protest, recognising a generous gesture from a man whose work force seemed to regard him as being close to the saints he was named for. 'Don't let the men hear you, though,' he warned. 'They'd consider it disrespectful and over-familiar. Workers here aren't so emancipated as they are in England, Miranda'

She began to relax. The man seemed to breathe out confidence and capability; she felt it crossing the space between them like a tangible, reassuring force. He was impressive, he was talented, but—he was approachable. Benvenuto ... Ben ... The full name so Italian, the shortened version so English. Perhaps in time she'd be able to use it quite naturally. It was better than Gabriel, anyway. The Archangel Gabriel ... Saint of the Saints ...

'Now,' he said, 'tell me how you came to be studying in glass.'

Under his questioning she related the events of her childhood and teens. 'So after "A" levels I did a year's foundation course and then started working for my degree.'

'But I gather that glass sculpture is not obligatory at the college?'

'No. Far from it, but we all had to choose our own speciality in preparation for our finals. Everyone else was sailing along, all organised: blowing, enamelling, cutting, sand-blasting, lots of different angles. But not me. All my life I'd known what to aim for until eight months ago when I had to specialise. Then I came to a very abrupt halt.'

The clear eyes looked intently into hers. 'Your Mr Wardle told me you haven't had any real training in sculpture.'

'That's right. As a child I was interested in modelling with clay, but once I saw the inside of my great-uncle's works I forgot all about that. Then at Art "A" level I had to make a female figure, and again I felt drawn to sculpture, but I was so keen on glass I didn't take it any further. Somehow the three-dimensional aspect only made sense when at last I applied it to glass.'

'And now that you've decided, what is it about the art that appeals to you most strongly?'

She'd thought that out months ago. 'It's the fact that the glass can speak for itself, rather than be submerged beneath another technique. Cutting, engraving, enamelling and so on, they're all wonderful skills, but to me, they end up by being more important than the glass itself.'

At that Benvenuto fell silent, so that she had no way of knowing whether he agreed with her or whether he thought she was talking rubbish. He pursed his lips, leaned back in the chair, and surveyed her with those crystal-like eyes.

Then at last he said, 'About your finals. I've arranged that anything you make on your own here can be verified by the university authorities as your own work. Then through the EEC students' scheme your pieces will be acceptable to the college for your end of course show.'

'But that's marvellous! I was worried as to how I could put together a decent show and come here as well.'

He looked faintly amused. 'Not worried enough to refuse, though?'

She shook her head. 'No. Once you'd made the offer I never thought seriously of rejecting it. We'd had a series of lectures on modern Venetian glass, you see, so I knew a little about you.'

He sat opposite her in his working clothes, arms bare and sinewy, covered with dark hairs. His fingers were tapping the leather of the chair. It was easy just then to forget his reputation in the world of glass, and she thought the moment right to ask a vital question.

'Mr dei Santi,' she began, 'about the baby's head I made. It wasn't very good, was it?'

'Not very. Neither, for a novice, was it bad, though unlike the glass we produce here in that it was moulded. Did you not find that a very laborious procedure?'

'Yes,' she said feelingly. 'I have to tell you, though, that it came out much better than I deserved. I was inexperienced, I tried to do it all on my own, and it was a case of trial and error over and over again. In the end it was sheer good luck.'

'Maybe so,' he said calmly, 'but it was still far and away the best exhibit in the student section of the exhibition.'

That silenced her for a moment, but he waited, knowing she had something else to say. She wondered how to phrase her next question, but his mind seemed to run ahead of hers to divine exactly what was troubling her. 'You're wondering what I saw in the head that made me ask you to come here?'

'Yes,' she said flatly. 'I've never stopped wondering that for the last three months.'

'Are you always so modest, I wonder?' He gave her no chance to reply, but went on, 'Look, Miranda, I'm sure you know that any artist worthy of the name works on more than one level. There's the way of instinct and the way of reason; the conscious and the subconscious; the heart and the mind. Can you just accept that I followed my instincts when I asked about you? No—don't delve too deeply at this stage—don't analyse.' To her astonishment he echoed Bill Wardle's words. 'Don't underestimate yourself, Miranda.'

'I'm not,' she protested, 'but it does seem to me that I'll be getting a lot out of my stay here, and you'll be getting very little. I hope to gain experience, expertise, knowledge; yet I can't see what I can do for you in return.'

He stared at her blankly. 'I run a business here, not a philanthropic institution, so rest assured that the dei Santi enterprise will gain something from employing you. You see, I'm convinced that art must be international—universal—it must be shared in order to develop and grow. Over the centuries Venice has cut herself off from the rest of the world's glass-makers, and our work has suffered as a result. We've had periods when we were so inward-looking we became obsessed with past glories and neglected to look to the future. I want to change all that.'

For a long, bitter moment Miranda believed that this was the reason he'd brought her here—to prove that very point. She'd *known* it, known he must have some ulterior motive in bringing her here ... She began to feel slightly sick. She was a pawn, she thought numbly, a pawn in some power game he was playing to change his company's outlook.

Then he leaned forward and said, 'Trust me, Miranda. I have your interests at heart, as well as those of my firm and the EEC.'

She found herself watching his lips intently while they framed those words. It seemed mad that at a vital moment in her career she should be thinking, and not for the first time, that his mouth was incredibly good to look at. But such was the power of his personality, so compelling the direct glance in his eyes, that she found herself nodding and smiling, suddenly content to rest all her doubts and worries on his capable shoulders. He'd said, 'Trust me.' And, quite simply, she found that she did.

'Now,' he went on more lightly. 'What do you think of the glass on sale in Venice? The good stuff, I mean.'

'Superb,' she said at once. 'The traditional work is magnificent, and the modern pieces—the sculptures in particular—are terrific.'

'You mean the technique is terrific? The finish?'

'Yes. To me it's amazing. I thought the abstract pieces quite brilliant.'

'Mm. And what of the studies from life?'

'Lovely,' she said forcefully.

'But——?'

She made an effort to look away from him. He was incredible. He *could* read her eyes. 'They're really lovely,' she insisted awkwardly, staring out at the lagoon.

He waited, eyelids half-lowered in that way of his. 'I can't say any more,' she protested. 'How can I possibly criticise such work?'

'Just tell me how you saw it,' he said reasonably. 'I won't take it personally.'

'Oh—not dei Santi glass,' she said hastily. 'I don't mean yours. I haven't seen your modern stuff yet. The showroom was closed when I went there and you have only traditional pieces in the windows.'

'Yes,' he said impatiently, 'but what——?' he broke off as there was a knock at the door and Felicetta Balbi came in with a tray. He waited until she had gone and stared at the coffee pot as if it held some vital message. 'Well?'

'A few of the pieces I saw, some of those from life— not all of them, of course——' She felt the warmth creep up her cheeks, 'I thought perhaps they were a bit—slick.'

'Hah!' he shot out the syllable like a bullet. 'You found something lacking, then?'

'Yes.'

'Well, what?' he demanded. 'What? What was lacking?'

She squirmed deeper into her chair. 'Feeling,' she muttered at last.

At that he leapt from his chair and pulled her to her feet. Keeping hold of her wrists, he said, 'Miranda Brown, you and I will get along together very well.'

He turned her hands over and dropped a kiss on each upturned palm. Then he folded her fingers down as if to keep the kisses safe, and pushed her gently back into her seat. She sat there and stared up at him without speaking, conscious that she could still feel the warm imprint of his lips on her palms.

'Have a cup of coffee,' he said briskly, 'then we'll go over the works.'

The evening meals at Signora Gaspari's were delicious, designed for large appetites, and noisy with talk and laughter.

There were ten boarders round the big table, all of them involved in some craft or profession. Students in picture restoring, stone preservation, ecology, music, architecture; everybody spoke freely about their work. Even Antoine, the quiet Frenchman, contributed an occasional anecdote about his researches in the archives of the Venetian Republic.

The two Italians from Verona were in the orchestra of the Fenice theatre for the opera season, and regaled the others with tales of life behind the scenes. The two of them were self-appointed language teachers at meal times, and corrected everybody's grammar and pronunciation with great good humour.

By Monday evening Miranda was getting to know them all. Spiro, the Greek, was next to her again, his profile and pelt of curly hair making her feel that she was sitting beside a section of the Elgin Marbles in the British Museum. He talked non-stop in garbled Italian with a strong Greek accent, and seemed quite astounded when she couldn't understand a word of it.

On her right was the only other female, the French

girl, Danielle. Slender, almost bony, with glossy hair
and wide spaced dark eyes, she was studying antique
dress in one of the city museums as part of her course
on theatrical costume. Miranda thought she might
prove to be a kindred spirit, and hoped to get to know
her better.

She joined in the chatter from time to time, paid
polite attention to Spiro, but her mind was still in the
dei Santi glasshouse, and as soon as she'd finished she
excused herself and went up to her room to finish her
first letter home. She felt just a little forlorn as she
signed her name and put an extra big kiss at the end for
Bobby. What were they all doing at home at that
moment?

Impulsively she jumped up, grabbed her jacket and
ran downstairs. She needed a walk to help throw off the
tensions of the day; she needed to think in order to
clarify her ideas and impressions.

Once outside, her head full of the day's happenings,
she turned her back on the two bridges and headed
towards the Riva degli Schiavoni—the wide waterfront
promenade that would lead her to the Piazza.

That morning they had finished their coffee in dei
Santi's studio, and with the ease of long practice
Miranda bundled back her hair and tied it out of the
way with a bandana.

'Do you always do that?' he asked.

'Yes. If I'm actually at the furnaces I wear a cap as
well, or at least a band round my forehead. My hair's a
bit unruly, you see.'

'But very beautiful,' he said seriously. He walked to
the door and barred her exit with an arm raised against
the door frame. 'Miranda. I don't know what the
situation is like towards women in the glass industry in
Stourley, but over here you may encounter a little

hostility. There are few women here, and even they are Venetian and from glass-making families. Our society as a whole is very male-dominated—but perhaps you know that?'

She knew immediately that it was this issue that troubled him about employing her. He, of all people, was explaining that Italy was a male-dominated society. He should know! 'There's still some resistance to having women in the glass industry at home,' she told him.

'So I've heard. But I feel I should warn you that you may find it altogether more intense over here. It's one of the oldest crafts in Venice, and the men can be very touchy about sharing what they regard as their heritage. They're militant—in the traditional rather than the trades union sense, and you're straight from college and young——'

She stretched her flat-heeled five foot three upwards. 'I'm almost twenty-three!'

'Yes,' he said resignedly. 'That's what I mean. Bill Wardle neglected to tell me your age. I'd expected someone older—more mature.'

He'd expected a mature student. No wonder he'd looked a bit stunned when he saw her. 'But whatever made you imagine that, Mr dei Santi? There are hardly any mature students on the entire course.'

'Something about the baby's head . . . oh, never mind . . . as long as you know what to expect. Let's go.'

She found it odd that such a decisive man should have kept postponing the moment when he talked to her about it. 'Don't worry,' she said gently. 'I've been in and out of glass works since I was a child.'

'I'm not worried,' he retorted, smiling faintly. 'Merely a little concerned on your behalf. I consider myself responsible for your welfare, don't forget.'

'I see,' she said blankly. 'I'm sure that's very kind of you, but there's really no need for it. I'm of age, and I can look after myself.'

'That remains to be proved,' he said drily. 'My father and I run this company jointly, you know, even though he has left Venice for health reasons. We discussed your arrival at length, and decided that the firm must treat its first foreign student well. With that in mind I've ensured that the men know you're here at my specific invitation, and that they must offer you full co-operation at all times.'

'Oh,' she said inadequately.

They went downstairs, and as if under compulsion Felicetta Balbi left her desk to watch them as they crossed the sunlit yard. The blonde English girl, small-waisted and slim-hipped, her hair swinging from its kerchief . . . it was odd how she kept her fingers tightly curled, as if keeping safe something in the palm of each hand . . .

As for the young Maestro, he was so like, and yet so unlike his father at the same age . . . Felicetta looked back across long, empty years and remembered another foreign girl arriving in Venice—a girl from America.

CHAPTER FOUR

MIRANDA walked on towards the waterfront, collar turned up and hands in pockets, feeling that she had been swept along by more chaotic emotions in her first day than in the whole of the past year at home.

When Benvenuto dei Santi led her into the works the first thing to strike her was how very similar it all was to an English glasshouse. The actual tools of the trade could have been English, and though the furnaces themselves looked every bit as ancient and dusty as they did at home, there was nothing remotely out of date in the sustained, powerful roar of their firing.

The teams of workers, or 'chairs' as they were called in England, moved back and forth in the calm, relaxed manner of men whose work cannot be hurried. And what work!

'Our traditional ware is made here, in the round-house,' explained her employer, making no attempt to interrupt them by introducing her, which was a relief. Some glanced at her curiously; others got on with their work and pretended she wasn't there, and a few of them watched her with the frank and open admiration which had so startled her on her first walk through the streets of Venice.

'We don't allow the public in here, unlike many of the firms,' said dei Santi. 'The work is too intricate to expect the men to concentrate with droves of tourists trooping in and out.'

Miranda was watching intently as the nearest 'chair' prepared for the next gather of glass from the crucible inside the furnace. 'I thought all glass works over here encouraged free access,' she said curiously.

'Many of them do, but you won't gain entry to firms working on high-grade pieces, or to those where large architectural fittings are made and assembled, and certainly not to those houses making originals or limited editions. Almost all dei Santi output is commissioned; a lot of it for the export trade. The rest of our work is sold through the showrooms you saw on the Grand Canal—our sole outlet in Venice.'

He would have moved on, but she was watching closely as a grey-haired man backed away from the white-hot glare of the furnace, a gather of glass on his rod. He twirled it gently as he carried it to his place, blowing down the rod in short, gentle bursts until the molten glass swelled and turned from vivid orange to dull red, and then he sat down in the long-armed 'gaffer's' chair that was so very like its English counterpart.

Miranda had often seen a vase formed, but this time there were subtle differences to look out for. The group of men walked backwards and forwards in a sequence of orderly, ritualised moves. One picked up a pliable gas pipe and played a jet of white flame on the curve of the vase; a young bit-boy stood patiently behind the chair waiting for his moment of action; while another man was at the furnace, checking the crucible, or pot, in readiness for the next gather of glass.

The gaffer rolled his rod back and forth on the slab of iron at the side of his chair; the bit-boy stepped forward and smartly knocked off the hardened end of the glass. The gaffer detached his rod and stood the still pliable glass on a metal slab, and with a grave, contemplative expression proceeded to flute the lip of the vase with hand-held pinchers. A man measured it with calipers against a drawing pinned to a board, and a fourth man went to a bench and sat there, arms folded, calmly waiting for the next move in the ritual.

Her employer's hand under her elbow urged her on past a chair making the world-famous Venice 'filigree'—the pale glass striped with fine, milky-white lines—and she hovered there, reluctant to leave, witnessing the infinite skill which combined the clear and the opaque glass with such precision.

After that, one impression seemed to merge rapidly into another. There was the glow from the furnaces touching dei Santi's face with gold; the men of each chair in their boldly-checked shirts, acknowledging her presence with restraint or else ignoring her completely; the superb equipment in all departments; the long, curved outer room that housed the sand and soda, the sacks and drums of chemicals and all the dry constituents of top-grade glass, and there was Innocenzo Paulucci, always within touching distance, his dark eyes restlessly seeking hers.

By her side Benvenuto reeled off facts and figures and statistics about glass-making, many of which she'd known for years, then led her to another building. 'This is where we assemble our big architectural commissions,' he said. 'Glass screens, chandeliers, ceiling diffusers, et cetera. They're usually designed for particular settings in public buildings.'

Fascinated, Miranda looked up at a series of roof-high gantries from which were suspended hundreds of semi-transparent glass rods. Of different lengths, they were graduated in colour from silvery-white, through gold and amber to a dull, coppery bronze. Against the utilitarian backdrop of packing-cases and criss-crossed girders the cascading mass looked enchanting.

Eyes huge with admiration, Miranda looked up at her employer. 'It's magnificent,' she breathed. 'But— what exactly is it, Maestro?'

That word! It had been on the tip of her tongue more than once since they entered the works. She'd known she would have to use it some time, but at the sight of this incredible creation it just came out naturally.

Instead of answering her he hesitated. She saw his teeth catch at his lower lip, while his gaze lingered absently on her face, as if his mind was elsewhere. 'It's a modern chandelier in the making,' he said at last. 'Or as they call it nowadays an "architectural illumination". To the men something like this is known familiarly as "*le forniture*" or "the fittings". This place, for instance, is known throughout the works as "the fittings shop".' He gestured towards the glass, using the graceful flick of the wrist which was essentially Italian. 'And the chandelier is for a new opera house in the States.'

'It's to be shipped to America?' Miranda couldn't imagine anything less likely, but he nodded.

'Our men will go over to assemble it. This particular piece will be of enormous size and weight, of course. Remind me to show you the architect's design.'

'But—do you often do this sort of work?'

'Constantly,' he said, and she caught a half hidden smile at her amazement. 'We've always specialised in lighting here in Venice, you know.'

Just then a gangling man in a formal suit hurried towards them. 'Maestro—the telephone—Copenhagen. They insist on speaking to you.'

'Oh all right. I'd better have a word. Please excuse me, Miranda. Innocenzo—kindly escort the signorina over the rest of this section then show her back to my studio.

Innocenzo Paulucci promptly came forward. After dei Santi's excellent English it came as a shock to be addressed in rapid Italian, and though in the next half hour her admiration for dei Santi glass soared to new heights, her confidence in her own ability with the language received a severe shaking. Not only did Innocenzo speak at top speed, he used technical terms with which she wasn't yet familiar, introduced her to several barely-polite workmen who also spoke only Italian, and at the same time managed to flirt with her quite openly. If she asked a question she had difficulty in making herself understood, so that she became silent unless addressed directly.

At last she'd had enough, and decided to go back to her room, though she found it an effort to phrase the simple request to go back. At once he agreed, smiling widely and displaying his very white, very even teeth. It was unfortunate that on the way back they met two men who requested an introduction, which Innocenzo performed with even more ceremony than his employer. Miranda stood there feeling like an exhibit in Madame Tussauds, but managed to remain calm and pleasant, following their rapid speech with difficulty and trying to look as if she knew exactly what was being said.

At last they reached the offices, and saw Benvenuto dei Santi in the doorway deep in conversation with a man from the shop floor. She said goodbye to Innocenzo and went up the stairs with her head throbbing. She must have been mad to think she would be able to communicate easily with the work force. She opened the door and there, as if awaiting her return, were the four views from the windows, serene and timeless, offering escape from the noise and glare of the works. Calmer now, she went and looked out across the lagoon to the distant sea, considering. She'd made herself understood at the Gaspari dinner table, hadn't she? So why not here?

She smiled in self-mockery. It was only eleven o'clock on her first morning, and already she was getting edgy. 'You're a nit-wit, Miranda Brown,' she told herself scornfully, and went to cool herself with a wash.

She grimaced at her reflection. Her hair was escaping from its tie; tendrils were curling against her cheeks and

the long, tied-back locks were a mad riot of curls. Not
for the first time she thought seriously about having it
all cut off. She'd resisted the temptation so far because
she thought the spectacular wheat-coloured mane gave
her a sort of distinction, and anyway, it was fashionable
to have masses of hair. If she had it cut now, though,
Ben dei Santi might regard it as a grovelling attempt to
make herself look less feminine, and so more acceptable
to his men. No chance! She'd keep it as it was. In fact,
she might let it grow down to her waist.

The telephone rang. 'Miranda? If you come down
now we'll finish our talk before I start work.' The
receiver was replaced before she could reply.

She snatched off the bandana, gave her head a
violent shake that set her hair spiralling wildly, and ran
down the two flights of stairs.

'How did you get on after I left you?' he asked as
soon as she entered the room.

'All right, I think,' she replied guardedly. 'The work
is stunning, but I'm nowhere near as good with the
language as I'd hoped. I think it would be better if
you'd speak only Italian to me in future. I can see that I
need to work at it much harder.'

He waited for her to sit down. 'I think you're doing
pretty well,' he said. 'But if you'll feel happier we'll
change over.' As soon as he spoke in his own tongue
she felt again that ridiculous sense of loss, as if her one
link with home had gone; but at least he spoke slowly
and very clearly.

'I think you should spend at least a week as an
observer only,' he said decisively. 'Go anywhere you
like in the works; watch the men, make notes, absorb it
all, and put down on paper any ideas you have on
design. I've gone through your sketches—they're
certainly different, and very original. Watch the glass,
apply your imagination to it, and see what you can

come up with in actual designs. Then next week we'll talk at length about a programme of work for you.'

'Right,' she said, somewhat stunned.

'Now, I expect you're puzzled as to why you haven't seen any sculptures?'

'Yes,' she said, wondering if her entire contribution to this talk was to be words of one syllable.

'The fact is that sculpture is a small and relatively new part of our work here, although I've experimented with it for some years. The usual sequence of events is that I plan something, work it out in detail, and then use one of the furnaces in the round-house, usually number four with Armani and his chair. I've arranged a job there for one o'clock today, immediately after the lunch break, and I think you'll find it interesting.'

At once Miranda recalled his phone call to the unknown Elena. This job he'd arranged was the reason for not lunching with her at the Danieli, wasn't it?

He handed her a rough sketch of a racing yacht, skimming with bird-like grace over the ocean. 'We're doing this today,' he said. 'A special commission for a yacht club in Newport, Rhode Island. The prototype— our first effort—is due out of the lehr this morning.' He shot her a keen glance. 'You'll know that the annealing is of crucial importance in making large pieces?'

'Oh yes,' she said feelingly, 'I know that only too well.' The annealing, or cooling of the glass, took place in a cooling tunnel called a lehr, and was a factor that had caused her constant anxiety with her own pieces at the college.

'You'll be able to learn more about that while you're with us,' he said. 'You can examine the prototype before we start work on the final version with Armani. He's just about my best man, and for some reason he's always known by his surname. All the rest—Tommaso,

Carlo, Lorenzo are given their Christian names, but Armani is—well—he's Armani.'

He gathered up a pile of papers. 'Can you find something to do now? Felicetta will be getting restless if I don't deal with the mail.' He walked to the door with her. 'Oh, by the way, I've told Baldassare to take you home this evening. I may be busy elsewhere.'

'But I can go on my own, by *vaporetto*,' she protested. 'I'm sure Baldassare has other things to do.'

'No doubt,' he said drily, 'but he's a dei Santi boatman and it happens to be me who pays his wages, so he does what I tell him. Besides, he seems quite taken with you.'

Miranda was quite taken with Baldassare, come to that, but she didn't say so. 'Off you go now,' he said abruptly. 'See you at one.'

Then, because he'd devoted the better part of his morning to her, she turned and gave him her wide, spontaneous smile. 'Thanks, Mr dei Santi,' she said sincerely. 'Everything I've seen has been absolutely marvellous.'

He didn't reply, but stood facing her on the landing, hesitating with surprising indecision. He touched her arm lightly with cool fingers, and then said an odd thing. 'Miranda, remember you're answerable only to me.' With a nod of the head he ran down the stairs and she heard him calling for Felicetta Balbi.

Armani had clever blue-green eyes that scrutinised her curiously from his wrinkled walnut of a face. 'The Maestro will be here in two minutes,' he said, darting a glance at the clock, 'but he told me you may see the design.' He unlocked a wall cupboard and took out a drawing, which he passed over reluctantly.

Miranda looked from the design to the prototype, newly out of the lehr. To her, the yacht looked perfect in its flawless blue-grey glass, and much bigger than she'd expected, almost a metre in height. The symbolic, bird-like grace demanded by the designer had been captured with great skill. She could see it was free formed, modelled from the molten glass rather than blown or poured into a mould, and she wondered why this one wasn't considered good enough for the commission.

'It is extremely beautiful, Signor,' she told Armani.

He looked at it critically and shook his head. 'The Maestro is not yet satisfied,' he said flatly. 'The sails— they are not filled out sufficiently, so the blowing of the wind, the sensation of speed—it is not conveyed. We will improve on it today.' He narrowed his eyes. 'You are to watch?'

'Yes,' said Miranda firmly. 'The Maestro has ordered it.'

He shrugged. 'So.' Apparently that was enough for the gnome-like little man. His furnace was roaring, his men were ready and waiting; the 'marver'—a great iron slab—was in position beside the long-armed chair.

Closely followed by Innocenzo, punctual almost to the second, Benvenuto dei Santi arrived and action commenced. Miranda, in her well-worn dungarees, sat perched on the wooden safety rail from where she had a grandstand view.

Four men carried the glass from the furnace on punty rods, and rolled it on the marver to a rough oval shape. Then, to Miranda's intense excitement, dei Santi grasped two short metal rods and calmly began to manipulate the molten glass into the first semblance of the body and sails of a racing yacht. From the start it was clear that he and not the older man was the expert on this piece of work. He communicated by means of outlandish calls and small gestures. 'Aye-ah . . . Oh-o-hay . . .' A flick of the wrist . . . a lift of the shoulder.

For the first time in her life Miranda saw the stately, measured tread of the glass workers become agitated. One man jumped up on a platform, ready to operate a block and tackle. Another hurriedly fastened the glass to the lifting gear, which then pulled and stretched part of it upwards. Dei Santi curved the hull, sharpened the bows and issued directions by deep-throated calls to the men.

Miranda sat on the rail, elbows on knees and her chin on her hands. She knew this glass would stay workable for much longer than Black Country lead crystal.

'Attenti!' called dei Santi suddenly to the men on the pulley, and they fell to making tiny, cautious movements.

'Basta!' grated Armani when the hull was narrowed enough.

The intense heat of the glass was affecting them all. Even Armani, shrivelled and apparently fleshless, was perspiring freely; while dei Santi's hairy chest was beaded with sweat as he eased more curve into the sails.

The work proceeded at speed. This was what excited Miranda about free-formed glass. It was immediate—formed in the heat of the moment. Molten glass waited for no man—or woman. It must be dealt with on the instant, for good or ill. There was no re-working, no altering, no time for adjusting.

At last the pace slowed. Innocenzo took a belated part and checked the measurements with the prototype, and there, against the furnace's glare and the sweating men, Miranda watched the glass fade until its own blue-grey colour emerged in the slender, impressionist form of an ocean-going yacht, racing before the wind.

She stayed perched on the rail, her heart wrenched with wonder and admiration. This was what it was all about—the creation of something so beautiful, so true, so unique, from the fusion of sand, soda and lime—the 'flux' that lay inertly in its sacks on the floor of the long curved room behind her.

Ben dei Santi was still in the chair, crouched over the glass. She could see only his big, confident hands and hairy forearms, his unbuttoned shirt and the top of his head. The thick black hair had lost its smoothness, and was springing up in a damp, unruly halo round his head.

The other chairs were all busy at work, while Armani's men moved at their Maestro's bidding, totally involved with the job on hand. Only Miranda was free. She watched her employer and became conscious of a strange sensation beneath her ribs, as if her heart had moved position of its own accord, and was attempting to break free from its casing of flesh and sinew. He really *was* a master of his craft, she told herself jubilantly, and he'd chosen *her* to come and work for him.

Just then he looked up for an instant and found her eyes fixed on him. He lifted his brows as if to ask, 'Well, what do you think?' Purely on instinct, she answered by inclining her head in a solemn tribute to his skill. He seemed to know what she meant, because he smiled at her, briefly and brilliantly, before bending his head to his work again.

Those heart-moving moments were with her still as she walked the Riva degli Schiavoni. Behind her a white cruise liner was berthed, lights ablaze, its passengers ashore exploring Venice, while across the water shone the island church of San Giorgio Maggiore, serenely floodlit against the evening sky, its bell tower reflected in the water.

She walked on, half her mind back on Murano, the other half taking in the brilliant scene around her; the dark waters, the golden lamps, and the lively, chattering crowds. At that moment a man and a woman emerged from a building just ahead, and laughing together at some shared joke made for a blue launch that dipped at a white mooring post.

It was the gold crest on the launch's cabin that halted Miranda. Only when she'd recognised the leaping flame and crossed blowing rods of the dei Santi did she pay attention to the couple. The man was Benvenuto dei Santi, immaculate in evening dress and looking very different from the sweating craftsman of the afternoon, and his companion, Miranda knew, could only be Elena, the woman he'd called 'my pretty one'.

She was more than pretty—she was beautiful—with coppery hair upswept in artful disarray and a classically oval-shaped face, at that moment lit by laughter. She was wearing a long black dress beneath a jacket of creamy fur and Miranda glimpsed fragile gold sandals on her feet; no wellingtons for her, she thought, even though the tide was almost at its height. Perhaps she was accustomed to being carried over the floodwater . . . after all, her companion was something of an expert at it.

She stood in the shadows and watched the two of them board the launch, presumably on their way to the theatre. They zoomed away in a whirl of spray, and she was left outside the ochre-coloured building they'd just left. It was the Danieli, where Benvenuto would no doubt have lunched with his 'pretty one' had he not arranged a job with Armani and his team . . .

Hands in the pockets of her chord jacket, she trudged on towards the Doges Palace. Behind the great creamy-pink building ran a narrow waterway, spanned by a small, roofed bridge. She recognised it at once. It was the *Ponte dei Sospiri*—the Bridge of Sighs.

Miranda stood there, her back to the open water where Benvenuto dei Santi's launch had by now disappeared. This was her first view of the Bridge of Sighs, and for some reason it seemed entirely appropriate to breathe a small sigh of her own.

CHAPTER FIVE

THERE was much talk during the evening meal at Signora Gaspari's. The two young musicians had been promised first refusal of a block of returned tickets for gallery seats at the Fenice theatre, and after that afternoon's rehearsal had triumphantly brought them home. Six tickets—one for each guest except the two Dutchmen, who were both jazz fanatics.

Miranda was touched that she'd been included so readily, and delighted at the propect of attending the fabled Fenice, especially for a gala performance of Verdi's *La Traviata*. They all decided to share a late supper after the opera, but Spiro didn't join in discussing the arrangements. He was busy juggling with the tickets before handing them round, ensuring that he would sit next to Miranda.

After the meal she went up to her room to sort out some revision, and much later Danielle joined her for the hot chocolate served ritually each evening at ten. Outnumbered four to one by the men, the two girls were fast becoming friends, and conversed in an experimental jumble of French, English and Italian.

At ten-thirty Danielle fluttered kohl-darkened eyelids, gathered her jellaba around her, and glided to the door. Miranda knew that as part of her course the other girl sewed a variety of costumes at lightning speed. 'I take it you're dealing with Eastern dress at the moment?' she asked, smiling.

Danielle uttered the squeak which, with her, passed for a giggle. 'Yes. And just wait till you see my harem trousers and yashmak,' she said.

*   *   *

It was Friday. Miranda sat at her window gazing across the lagoon and eating her solitary lunch. Thoughtfully she munched an apple and poured herself more coffee, reflecting on her first week at work.

The days had passed as decreed by her employer; she'd been an observer only, though free to wander at will through the glasshouse. She'd seen superb pieces being made, watched the flux being measured, the immense architectural fittings assembled, the lehrs loaded under the watchful eye of the diminutive Carlo, and throughout it all had met with a total lack of co-operation from the workforce.

Under their Maestro's orders, the men had been scrupulously polite, creating the impression of being helpful while in fact being quite the reverse. It had taken her until late on Tuesday to see that she was being obstructed every inch of the way, and by mid-day on Wednesday she'd stopped carrying her notebook, sensing the hostility provoked by her rapid scribbling.

She stared at the distant domes and bell-towers of Venice and shook her head disbelievingly. Did they imagine she would rush home to the Black Country, brandishing a notebook of trade secrets, and single-handedly transform the lead-crystal industry into a replica of Murano? She was a student, for heaven's sake, not an industrial spy. Benvenuto dei Santi's warning to her had been clear enough, but at the time she'd made light of it. She should have known he wouldn't exaggerate the reactions of his men.

Already she had a shrewd idea of the struggle facing her, and would have felt isolated and quite despondent had it not been for the guarded overtures of Felicetta Balbi and the friendship of the ever-attentive Innocenzo. So often did she and the young Italian come face to face in the works she began to imagine he must keep lookouts posted to warn him of her approach. She couldn't bring herself to like him, though. He was too sure of his attractions, too brashly masculine in spite of his incredible eyes and perfect features; but at least he was friendly and cheerful, and in that hostile atmosphere he boosted her tottering morale.

Surprisingly, he made no attempt to visit her studio. Only her employer and his secretary climbed the stairs in the tower. The small grey-haired woman with her quick, neat movements and quiet smile appeared once a day, made polite small talk, checked that Miranda had everything she needed, and at the end of five minutes would depart as abruptly as she'd arrived.

Of Benvenuto himself Miranda had seen little since that first, memorable day. On Tuesday he'd picked her up at Celestia and zoomed across a stormy lagoon after stowing her away in the cabin out of the rain. She had watched his rear view and wondered how the glamorous Elena had enjoyed her birthday outing. After that, at her own request, she'd travelled back and forth on public transport, to find that the crowded passenger boat made a poor substitute for the comfort and speed of the dei Santi launch.

Through the week he sometimes asked a quick question of her in passing, ran up the stairs to give her a rapid word of encouragement, directed at her an all-seeing stare from the brilliant eyes if they met in the works, and performed formal introductions between her and key men on the shop floor. That was all.

Yet even when she saw nothing of him for hours on end, the knowledge that he was backing her gave her confidence in facing his men. He might be bossy, even domineering at times, but to her, in that alien environment, his concern for her well-being acted like some kind of armour, protecting and enfolding her. When she recalled his acute discomfort at the prospect of her encountering hostility, she felt again that peculiar lifting of her heart.

Now, instinctively, she rejected the idea of going to him for advice on how to overcome the prejudice of the workers. Beyond her desire to please him, to prove him right in bringing her here, lay her devotion to glass and her tough, Midlands determination. She might not be God's gift to Murano, but neither was she a little blonde tweet-tweet. She could work—she *would* work—she'd show them what English girls were made of. She resolved to have won them over by the end of her four weeks' probation, and she ringed the deadline on her calendar—the third Friday in May.

As for the work itself, she would set aside part of each day for sketching. There was no resident designer, so she would dream up a few ideas of her own. After all, Benvenuto dei Santi had told her to 'watch the glass, apply her imagination to it, and see what she could come up with'. Very well, she'd do just that.

And what was more she'd ask him for furnace-time in order to attempt a few small pieces of her own for her show back at the college. Perhaps he would let her use number six, so that she'd be behind the partition there, away from the critical eyes of the men . . .

Conveniently ignoring the immense practical skill needed to make anything at all, let alone something of merit all on her own within feet of the dei Santi craftsmen, Miranda felt her spirits rise. A girl from Stourley wasn't going to be intimidated by a bunch of skilled men in Venice!

Late that afternoon she heard rapid footsteps on the stairs and then Benvenuto appeared at her open door. She knew he'd been experimenting with different mixes to find a new, subtler shading for a batch of glass, so she wasn't surprised at the state he was in. A film of fine, silver dust lay over his hair, his eyebrows, and the dark chest hair beneath his unbuttoned shirt. He looked irritable and as if he had no time to spare for idle chit-chat; but when he spoke it was with his customary courtesy, and in English, although as usual he went straight to the point.

'Miranda, I wonder if you're free on Saturday evening? I'm taking a party of friends to the gala performance of *Traviata* at the Fenice, and I thought you might care to join us?'

She'd been tidying up her work-bench when he appeared, and she still held scraps of gold-flecked glass rescued that morning from Armani's bit-box. Cheeks pink, her hair escaping from an untidy knot on top of her head, she looked up at him and felt both relief and regret.

'I'm sorry, Mr dei Santi, but I've already arranged to go to the Fenice with friends.' And then, telling herself that the man seemed to know what would appeal to her in Venice, then took the trouble to provide her with it, she smiled at him warmly and said, 'Thanks a lot for asking me, though. I do appreciate it.'

He lifted one shoulder and said coolly. 'I have a spare seat in my box, that's all. It seemed a pity to waste it. The tickets were sold out weeks ago, so you're fortunate to have obtained one.' He tapped his fingers on the end of the workbench. 'These friends you're going with. Do I know them?'

She stared at him blankly. 'No, I don't imagine you do. Why?'

He sighed audibly. 'Because, as I've told you already, I'm responsible for you while you're over here, working with me. Half the weirdos and drop-outs of Europe pass through Venice at some time or other, and I can't have you going around with anyone of that kind. Surely you see that?'

Miranda saw something else. He was back to square one, being as bossy as the devil. She tucked a few wayward locks of hair behind her ears and stretched upwards another half inch; then directed her gaze straight ahead and found herself staring at the dust-touched black hairs at the base of his throat. She reminded herself that though he was half-American, he lived in the male-dominated society of Italy, and was merely acting in accordance with the creed of his home country. Be that as it may, *she* was British.

'I don't recall signing any agreement with you other than the one relating to my employment,' she said edgily. 'Have I inadvertently signed away my rights to use my leisure time as I see fit, and in the company of those friends I choose?'

'Oh, don't talk like a child,' he said unfairly. 'Nobody signs anything "inadvertently" for me, least of all when it concerns their rights.' He lifted a hand and sighed again. Like a man hedged around by trivia when he has important work to be done. 'All right—don't tell me—you're of age. I know that. And I know all about the independence of the British.' He shook his head. 'I don't want to quarrel with *you*, Miranda.'

She fancied that his emphasis on the 'you' meant that though he might well quarrel with someone in authority, he couldn't be bothered to quarrel with anyone as insignificant as her. 'I'm not quarrelling,' she retorted, 'merely making clear that I don't want my personal life to be monitored, that's all.'

He made no reply, but just stood there, looking over her head expectantly. She thought rapidly. It was solely due to this man that she was in Venice. If he wanted to be awkward he could send her back to Stourley in three weeks' time without having taught her a single thing about glass sculpture. She couldn't afford to antagonise him, even over a matter not connected with work, and in any case a two-minute argument wasn't going to change all this stuff about being responsible for her.

She bit her lip, hesitating. It was surprisingly painful to be at odds with him—or maybe not surprising at all considering he was her sole ally in this place, except, possibly, for Innocenzo. At last she said, 'Two of Signora Gaspari's guests are members of the orchestra at the Fenice, and they managed to get hold of six returned tickets for the first gallery. The five friends going with me are students: two French, a Greek, a German and a Belgian. Four of them male, one female.'

'That's all I wanted to know,' he said mildly. 'Why all the fuss? Maybe I'll see you up there in the gallery, far above me.'

Then she said something that really was childish. 'I'll wave to you,' she promised gravely.

At that he smiled. The smile that was so rare and so bedazzling that it brought to her mind a shaft of sunlight on untouched snow, or the white-hot light of a furnace at maximum heat. Two opposite extremes of temperature, and somehow he put her in mind of both.

He reached out a hand and touched her firm, slightly grubby chin. 'And I'll wave back to you,' he replied. With a chuckle he turned, ran back down the stairs and returned to the works, leaving Miranda still holding the scraps of glass in her cupped hands, like an offering.

She walked out through the gates that Friday, relieved to have the weekend ahead, and feeling vaguely uncomfortable about the modest wages handed to her in private by Felicetta Balbi. It seemed to her that she'd done little to earn them, unless putting up with the attitude of the men merited payment.

On every side the glass-makers of Murano were heading for home. Sturdy men, relaxed and confident, some of them with the fair skin and light brown hair which had proved wrong her imaginings that all Italians were black-haired and swarthy. A few of them eyed her with open admiration, but the majority stared with unsmiling curiosity. Had they heard that dei Santi had an English girl working for him? She shrugged and walked on. If they didn't know already they would very soon hear of it in the bars and cafés of the waterfront.

She passed the little market where fish and vegetables were on sale each morning beneath the columned overhang of an old house. After five days on Murano she'd seen nothing of the island except the quayside, this road, and the view of the rooftops from her room in the tower. Perhaps in future she'd take a picnic snack and spend her lunch-hours exploring.

Waiting with the crowd at the landing-stage she felt someone touch her arm. It was Baldassare Antelami, bulky and reassuringly friendly. 'I am taking goods to the railway freight yard, and I see you waiting here. Can I offer you transport to the Gaspari house?'

'Why thanks, Signor. I'd be delighted.'

They headed out to the lagoon while he made detailed enquiries as to her health and that of her parents; then he asked, 'And how does the signorina like to be employed by the establishment dei Santi?'

Miranda hesitated. He was one of the work force, after all, and probably felt about her much as the other men did. 'It's all a bit strange just yet,' she admitted carefully, 'but I'm very impressed by the quality of the work.'

'It is good,' he agreed. 'The Maestro, he has great talent, both in making the glass and in running the business. As for you, Signorina, your skill in our language will no doubt be of help to you in the glasshouse?'

At his question Miranda raised wary eyes to his, fighting the urge to confide in this kind, reliable-seeming man.

'I have three sons and a daughter,' he announced suddenly. 'My daughter is of an age with you, and is soon to be married.'

'Oh.' Miranda was slightly nonplussed. 'That's splendid. I also have three brothers.'

'You look not unlike my daughter,' he went on, 'but she is dark, you understand, and does not have hair like the sunshine. I should worry about her if she was in a foreign country among strangers. I am concerned for her welfare at all times.'

And then Miranda understood. He was telling her in his own way that she could trust him, that he was concerned about her. She smiled in a rush of relief. 'I understand, Signor. Thank you.'

'So,' he persisted, 'you have no trouble with the language?'

'It's not easy,' she admitted. 'Everyone speaks so rapidly I can hardly follow what they say. But I'm working on it.'

Baldassare steered, one-handed and impassive, towards an oncoming work barge. 'Does Innocenzo Paulucci not help you?' he asked.

'Innocenzo? Not really. He's kind, but I can't follow him any better than the others.'

The boatman nodded to himself. 'But Paulucci speaks excellent English, Signorina. He is second only to the Maestro in the spoken word, and helps to train the saleroom staff in the language.'

Their boat rocked wildly in the wake of the barge, and Miranda felt as if her mind was in a similar upheaval. She looked back on incidents throughout the week when a few words in English from Innocenzo could have made things immeasurably easier for her. 'Perhaps he thought that I was supposed to speak only Italian,' she said at last.

'Perhaps,' nodded Baldassare. 'Yes, perhaps that is so. Does the Maestro know of your difficulties?'

'He knows I was worried about it,' she said slowly, 'but naturally I didn't mention Innocenzo in particular. I just asked the Maestro to speak to me only in Italian so that I would become used to it more quickly.' She looked at the grey-haired figure next to her. 'You won't say anything to him about this, Baldassare? I don't want him to see me as a source of trouble.'

'Benvenuto dei Santi wanted you here,' said the boatman grimly, 'therefore he must not be too amazed if indeed you *are* a source of trouble, and not of your own making. He knows his men, you understand, therefore it follows that he must know of their feelings.'

A moment later they reached the long quayside of the Fondamente Nuove, and edged their way into the city canals towards Due Ponti. Miranda was silent, feeling tired and rather resentful. Surely Innocenzo couldn't have misunderstood about the language situation? He seemed so friendly, so anxious to help ... in fact, she'd been sure he fancied her, and had even wondered how she could give him the brush-off without denting his macho image too badly ...

They bumped gently to a halt between the two little bridges, and the boatman held out a big warm hand to help her alight. 'Signorina,' he said quietly, 'if ever the Maestro is absent and you need help—come to Baldassare.'

Need help, she thought, what sort of help? Coming from that stocky, sensible figure the words seemed oddly melodramatic; but then the Italian temperament did lean towards melodrama ... 'I will,' she promised, and on impulse leaned forward and kissed the weathered cheek.

'Oh ho!' he laughed, suddenly cheerful again. 'If Baldassare were only twenty years younger! Goodbye for now, little Mee-ran-dah.'

Feeling warmed by his concern, little Mee-ran-dah

opened the door of the tall pink house and ran up to
her room. She threw wide the shutters above the canal
and watched him head the boat towards the goods
yard. Their talk had given her plenty to think about,
but her mind clung obstinately to one particular phrase:
'Benvenuto dei Santi wanted you here . . .'

Wearing what she told herself was an utterly fatuous
smile, Miranda looked in the mirror, groaned at her
wild aureole of hair, then picked up a towel and went
singing to the bathroom.

Minutes later, her body hidden in the depths of the
immense bath, she stopped smiling. Benvenuto dei Santi
wanted her here, yes. But why? Again the unpleasant
thought came to her that he'd brought her here to prove
to his men and the glass industry in general that Venice
was changing her image, becoming one with the EEC,
and employing women . . . *foreign* women.

She finished her bath in silence, nearly falling back in
the tub head-first when she leaned over to wash it out.
Towelling herself, body still tense, she remembered
Benvenuto dei Santi's words on that first morning. He'd
said, 'Trust me, Miranda.' She stood there, naked, the
towel clasped to her breasts, quite unable to see him as
a man who would say that without meaning it. Instinct
battled with cold logic, and won. She *did* trust him.

A moment later Antoine Bonsart looked up from his
meticulous notes. Light footsteps passed his door, and a
slightly off-key contralto voice could be heard singing
'Greensleeves'. He smiled. They were all getting used to
Miranda's vocal repertoire.

The narrow streets and hump-backed bridges echoed
with the sound of countless footsteps. From all
directions people were converging on La Fenice, ablaze
for her gala performance.

Water-taxis jostled each other on the Rio della

Fenice, gondolas delivered groups of smiling tourists, and on the arms of their menfolk the elegant women of Venice drifted along on their four-inch heels, pleased to be showing off their finery.

The six young people lingered by the steps of the high-pillared entrance. As gallery patrons they themselves hadn't needed to dress up, but in honour of the occasion Miranda wore her frilly pink blouse with a mulberry cotton skirt, and Danielle sported the harem trousers with a beaded top, but had refrained from adding the yashmak.

'Come on. Let's go.' Klaus wasn't one to hang about, and he was impatient to lay claim to their seats. The six of them trooped round the corner and entered by a modest side door, then climbed long flights of stairs.

Their seats were on the front row, and Miranda leaned over the balustrade, enchanted by the auditorium. The tiers of seats were lit by hundreds of little lamps between delicately painted panels edged in gold. Each separate level was divided by identical pillars and drapes to create the illusion that the entire theatre was made up of private boxes, so that despite the splendour it retained an air of intimacy and warmth.

Far below the orchestra was tuning up and the audience occupying their pink velvet seats. Miranda shook her head. She'd never spot Benvenuto dei Santi in that throng, let alone wave to him. As for their two musical friends, they were with the other woodwind players, out of sight in the orchestra pit.

Spiro was tugging at her hand to urge her to sit down. The young Greek looked vaguely apprehensive, and Miranda guessed he would have felt more at home in a disco or one of his native tavernas. Then the conductor made his entrance and everyone fell silent for the overture. It was a supremely polished production; very different, she suspected, from the opera's première

long ago in this very theatre—a performance described
by Verdi himself as 'a fiasco'.

The tragic love story, based on Dumas' *Lady of the
Camellias*, was sung and acted with immense skill and
feeling, and she loved every minute of it. At the first
interval the others went off in search of drinks, but
Miranda stayed where she was, still under the spell of
her first live opera. She leaned forward and looked
below, but most of the seats were empty.

During the next act Klaus handed her his opera
glasses, and in her attempts to focus on the singers she
suddenly found herself studying in close-up a lovely
oval face beneath piled-up coppery hair. It was the
woman Elena, wearing a low-cut topaz coloured dress
and sitting in a box close to the stage. Even before she
moved the glasses Miranda knew who would be her
companion, but there were several of them: a young
boy with curly hair and an older man and woman.
Then, for a moment, the tenor's pure impassioned notes
were lost on her as she saw the other occupant of the
box. It was, of course, Benvenuto dei Santi, leaning
back in his seat with a hand outstretched to touch the
back of Elena's chair.

His attention was on the stage, and for all of two
minutes Miranda watched him through the powerful
glasses. He looked quite incredibly attractive in evening
clothes, relaxed and yet serious, and with lips parted
Miranda pressed the glasses closer to her eyes, seizing
this unique opportunity to observe him. What exactly
was he thinking as he watched the stage where Alfredo
was so passionately in love with his Violetta?

Klaus nudged her to pass on the glasses and she
obliged, feeling annoyed with herself at the way she'd
studied so intently that lean, unaware profile. There had
been an empty chair next to him—as far as she could
see the only unoccupied seat in the theatre. It was

fortunate for her that she wasn't sitting in it, considering she'd spent part of the time sniffling back tears and didn't own a single item of clothing that was remotely suitable.

The act came to an end. She saw everyone in the box join in the applause, and then Benvenuto lean forward to speak to Elena. Even without the glasses she could see his lips move in speech only inches away from the bare, glistening shoulders. Was he in love with her? Was she in love with him?

Before they climbed the steps she turned for a last look at the dei Santi box. The others had disappeared, but he was still there, opera glasses to his eyes, focusing on the gallery. 'That's Mr dei Santi!' said Miranda to nobody in particular, and leaned forward and waved. Far below her the Venetian picked up his programme and waved back, long and deliberately.

In the warm glow of the theatre lights she saw the gleam of his smile, the sheen of his hair, and even, so she imagined, the glitter of those crystal-like eyes. And then Spiro's hand behind her waist urged her on, and with a last look over her shoulder she let him lead her away.

The last act was touching beyond belief, and then all too soon it was over and the audience on its feet. Over the years the Venetians had made generous amends to Verdi for their original reception of Traviata. The curtain calls continued for ten minutes before the lights went up and everyone prepared to leave.

They clattered down the stone steps, and as they followed the crowd into the narrow street outside, a tall figure in evening dress stepped forward. For the second time in a week Miranda greeted her employer with a dismayed 'Oh!'

Apparently unperturbed, he bent his head in greeting and looked at the others in bland expectancy, waiting to

be introduced. Miranda almost ground her teeth. For
goodness sake, he'd come *to inspect them*! Obviously he
wasn't yet convinced that they weren't 'the drop-outs of
Europe'.

So, jostled by departing crowds, she introduced her
five companions, using Christian names only for the
very good reason that she wasn't sure of their surnames.
'May I present my friends—Danielle, Klaus, Spiro,
Maurice and Antoine—this is my employer, Benvenuto
dei Santi.'

They all murmured politely, in no hurry to move on
as they had to wait for their two friends from the
orchestra. Then Miranda was intrigued to see the dei
Santi charm switched on at full power. He asked if
they'd all enjoyed the performance, and if they agreed
with him that Verdi had been a man of genius; he said
how delightful it must be for Miranda to have friends of
so many nationalities, and in two minutes flat made it
clear to her that the other five had passed muster. She
began to wonder if he intended to stay chatting all
night. 'Are your party not with you?' she asked.

'No, they're still inside,' he answered carelessly.
'There's some sort of meal arranged with the singers—
to celebrate the end of the opera season. I just came out
here to have a brief word with you. Could you come to
my place tomorrow morning for half an hour or so, to
discuss how you are to spend next week? I know it isn't
a working day, but we'll be uninterrupted away from
the glasshouse, and there's much to arrange.'

'Of course I'll come,' she said at once. 'What time?'

'About eleven? I'll pick you up.'

'No,' she said quickly. 'Please don't do that. I'll come
on my own. I'd rather.'

'As you wish.' The cool grey glance flicked to Spiro,
standing close behind her, then he kissed Danielle's
hand in farewell, to that young woman's evident

enjoyment, and for an instant held Miranda's fingers before touching them also with his lips. 'Tomorrow, then?'

'Yes,' and remembering his remark as they sailed down the Grand Canal, 'over the shop?'

'That's right. We open from ten until twelve on Sunday, so just go in and ask the sales staff for me.' He looked round the tight little group and said with quiet civility, 'It has been a great pleasure to meet you all. I bid you good night.'

Without a backward glance he walked away towards the main entrance, leaving Miranda to answer her friends' rather stunned enquiries about what he was like to work for.

CHAPTER SIX

MIRANDA stood beneath the arcades of the Piazza San Marco. The warning sirens had sounded hours before, and now she was waiting to see the waters flow in from the sea. When at last the flooding began she was surprised to see that it came, not from the waterfront, but bubbling up through gratings in the pavement of the Piazza itself. Of course . . . as the water rose it must flood the substructure before it overlapped the quay . . .

Trying hard not to smile with delight at the sight of what the Venetians must regard as a positive nuisance, Miranda walked round the perimeter of the great square and watched the water spread outwards from its centre. Raised boardwalks were already in place, and when it was almost ten o'clock she joined the trooping lines of worshippers entering the Basilica, and stood out of sight behind a marble column, watching High Mass.

The vast interior was incredible, she thought, its domes gleaming with gold mosaics and its priceless relics of Byzantium. She stood there, listening to the music and watching the congregation move forward to receive Communion; wealthy Venetians in fur coats and prosaic wellingtons mingling with tourists in anoraks and old ladies in sombre black and galoshes. The priests moved back and forth in front of the great rood screen, while high above them were ranked dark and very dusty statues of the Virgin and Apostles. The irreverent thought came to Miranda that if Betty was with her she would be in a positive frenzy to get at them with a duster.

Silently she edged towards the door. San Marco was

magnificent, with its Eastern treasures and its origins
lost in the mists of time, but it was so totally foreign
that she felt a strange dampening of her spirits, a
sudden longing for the serene familiarity of the little
parish church in Stourley.

Outside again the sun was dazzling and she splashed
along in her wellies with her collar turned up and her
hands deep in her pockets. Once on dry pavement
again she walked along the waterfront, pausing only
to look through the railings of the Reali Gardens to see
the cats. A colony of them, well-fed and sleek, inhabited
the shrubbery there, and she glimpsed their shadowy
forms in the undergrowth and saw three tabby kittens
playing together while their mother watched nearby.

She boarded a *vaporetto* to cross the Grand Canal,
heading for the great white church of the Salute, not far
from the dei Santi showrooms. The churches of Venice,
she thought, with their domes and their works of art
and their leaning bell towers, would she ever find time
to visit them all? No, said the sober voice of reason, not
if she was only here for another three weeks.

She tossed her head and her hair swirled wildly. What
was the point in speculating about that on such a
morning? The air smelt of the sea, the sun was shining,
the water was sparkling, and they were passing the
Dogana, the old customs house surmounted by its great
golden globe. Stepping ashore at the Salute, she made
her way through the maze of streets towards the dei
Santi showrooms.

The sales floor was superb, but she was given no
opportunity to examine the displays, because Benvenuto
dei Santi was already there, talking to an older man,
almost as if he was waiting for her. He was wearing a
dark suit with a silk shirt and tie, and at once Miranda
felt far too casual for a Sunday morning in Venice,

dressed as she was in her angora sweater and grey flannel skirt.

He launched forth on one of his introductions, and after repeat performances around the showroom ushered her briskly towards some stairs without letting her look at a single piece of glass. 'Later!' he said, waving an impatient hand. 'Come up to my apartment now. I have to be away by twelve.'

Two floors up, outside double doors, she removed her jacket and slipped into flat leather pumps from her bag. He led her into a spacious room, where faded silken rugs gave warmth to a floor of polished white marble. It was almost austerely bare, the furniture very old but simple in line and the walls dove grey with few pictures. Not surprisingly, there were four splendid glass chandeliers, which she was relived to see were relatively plain, with none of the florid ornamentation in which the old glassmakers had excelled.

She knew that the high Gothic windows must overlook an impressive stretch of the Grand Canal, but her attention was taken not by the view, but by a flexible glass screen set behind a group of sofas. They made such screens in the fittings-shop at the works, and on Friday she had watched them slatting the sections of one together . . . it had been grey-green . . . geometrically precise, and very beautiful . . . A nebulous idea from the back of her mind suddenly presented itself, sharply-detailed and complete. A glass screen in colours of the ocean; blues, greens, misty greys, its linking sections representing aquatic life—fish, shells, seaweed . . .

'Miranda?' He'd been speaking, but she hadn't heard.

'I'm sorry, Mr dei Santi. I missed that. It was seeing your screen. It set me thinking about this idea I had—er—it was nothing, really.'

The intent, analytical gaze was on her face. 'All I said was would you care to sit here?' He indicated one of the sofas, then crossed to the fireplace and pulled a bell-rope.

Miranda watched him silently. So people still did that in real life! Pulled a bell-rope to summon the minions. The plump lady who carried in a loaded tray hardly had an air of servility, though, and was introduced by him with some affection as, 'Signora Antelami, who is good enough to help in the house from time to time. The Signora is the wife of your friend, Baldassare, Miranda.'

She jumped up to shake hands, and saw that the round, good-natured face held the same down-to-earth kindliness as her husband's. The dark eyes looked into Miranda's blue ones, and her fingers reached out and touched the shining hair. 'Si, si,' she said. 'It is indeed like the sunshine!' She poured their coffee, bestowed on them a beaming smile, and, with visible reluctance, left the room.

'I've given my resident staff the day off,' he explained, making Miranda wonder if he'd brought in Signora Antelami merely to make a pot of coffee. Then, as if he hadn't been dragging her around at top speed, he plied her with tiny iced cakes and more coffee, leaned back in a leisurely fashion and said, 'Tell me how you're liking Venice, Miranda. Does the city come up to your expectations?'

'Oh, yes. It's utterly fascinating and—and gorgeous. The opera last night was terrific, and this morning I've seen the flood-water come bubbling up in the Piazza, and watched High Mass in San Marco.'

He was watching her with that odd expression she'd noticed before; perplexed but intent, like—she told herself—like a scientist confronted by a hitherto unknown species. Perhaps that was how he saw her!

Then he poured more coffee, and said, 'You find San Marco a little overpowering, perhaps?'

'Yes,' she admitted, surprised, 'I do. It's magnificent, but—let's just say it takes a bit of getting used to.'

He smiled faintly. 'You would like San Giorgio Maggiore on its little island. The interior is white, serene, and very plain. I've just been over there to hear the monks sing the Gregorian chant. I find it refreshing after a busy week. Have you been told from which vantage-point the best view of Venice is to be seen?'

'The bell tower in the Piazza?' she hazarded.

'No. Not in my opinion.' His tone indicated that no other opinion was worthy of attention, and Miranda concealed a smile. 'The best view in Venice is to be had from the tower of San Giorgio.' He swung one foot up and down and regarded his shoe thoughtfully. 'I'd like to show you that view myself, Miranda. Will you save it for me?'

'Yes,' she said, taken aback. 'Of course I will.'

'I'll tell you when the day is right,' he replied obscurely. 'Now—let's get down to business. Perhaps you've noticed that I've been rather busy this last week?'

The understatement of the year, thought Miranda. 'Yes. I've noticed,' she agreed.

'That's because I've been clearing up anything outstanding in order to reorganise my working week. From now on you and I will work together on both theory and practical skills for three hours every afternoon. The mornings will be yours to sketch, write up your notes, and go round the works watching the men. I've made clear to them that if you so wish you may even stand beside them at the furnaces.' He looked at her keenly. 'You've been in and out of glasshouses for long enough—you don't need a lecture on safety?'

'No,' she said.

He passed over a timetable, handwritten in his now familiar pointed script. 'This is what I've thought of to begin with. Tomorrow we go over what you've already learned about sculpture. Tuesday we start on simple free-formed shapes, abstracts, birds, fishes, that sort of thing. I'll make them, you watch until you're confident enough to try on your own. I'd like you to take home a selection of your own work that can be included in your show at the College. And each day we'll have a short session in the lab with Enrico. I seem to recall that you're proficient in physics and chemistry?'

'Yes, but Mr dei Santi, all this is going to take up an awful lot of your time. I really don't expect it.'

There followed one of the silences which sometimes fell between them, with Miranda waiting for his next remark and the Venetian staring at her without saying a word. She found it a bit unnerving.

Then he said, 'How have you been getting on with the men?'

She opened her mouth to make a non-committal reply, but instead blurted out, 'They don't want me here. You were right. They resent me.'

To her dismay she surprised on his dark features the look she'd seen there before: ill at ease, slightly guilty. He went to the windows and stared absently at the waterway below. 'No,' he agreed quietly. 'They don't want you here.' He swung round on her, 'But I do, Miranda. Remember that. *I* want you here, and what I say goes. If they don't like it, that's too bad.'

Fascinated, half-repelled, she recognised a determination, a ruthlessness, that was all the more worrying because she was the unwitting cause of it. She sensed the raw power behind that cool, high-handed statement.

He'd gone back to staring at the water, and she watched him thoughtfully. She knew her Venetian history, knew that more than a thousand years ago his distant ancestors had fashioned their infant state from a straggle of muddy islands in a lagoon; had moulded Venice, fought and schemed for her, until she merged as a glittering republic, wealthy beyond dreams, a supreme naval power who called herself the Serenissima and surveyed the rest of the world with haughty disdain.

His profile looked black against the brilliance of the April sky. No wonder they'd ruled the world if they were all like him, she thought rebelliously. But *he'd* brought her here from England. It was his problem. Let *him* sort it out.

'Listen to me,' he said at last. 'I know how it's been for you this week. Oh no—nobody's told me—least of all you. I've sensed what's been going on and made a few deductions of my own. Obviously we shall have to take it slowly with the men, because I can't afford to lose even one skilled craftsman——' Her eyes widened in alarm. Surely he didn't think—— 'We'll win them over by degrees,' he went on. 'We can't yet expect them to teach you anything, so I'm going to do it. *That's* why I'm giving you "a lot of my time", as you put it. I may not be a brilliant teacher, but I think I'll have an eager pupil. Yes?'

'Yes,' she said.

'Now. Tell me what's impressed you most out of what you've seen in the works.'

'The racing yacht,' she said promptly. 'I'm longing to see it come out of the lehr.'

'Hah!' He jerked his head back. 'You liked it? You shall see me polish it.' He sat beside her and picked up the timetable. 'It needs eleven days in the lehr, so it's due out on Friday. We'll spend an hour or so examining it and preparing it for polishing.'

Miranda sat there with his dark sleeve brushing hers, and felt a tremor of alarm. She would have to be in close contact with this man for the next few weeks ... What would her friends at college say when they knew that Benvenuto dei Santi was putting her under his personal tuition? She must write and tell them, and write to Bill Wardle as she'd promised . . .

'And what was this idea you had for a glass screen?'

She bit her lip. 'You did tell me to see what I could come up with,' she reminded him.

'I know I did. And I meant it. Well?'

'I envisaged this huge screen with an aquatic theme. Shells, fish, bubbles, and so on, all in muted sea colours, linked by ribbons of seaweed.' Heavens, it sounded revolting! 'That's all,' she finished lamely.

'You've heard then? Who told you?'

She stared at him. 'Heard what? Told me what?'

'That several firms have been asked to submit ideas for an ornamental screen. A commission with some prestige for whoever gains it.'

'No, I hadn't heard about that. How could I? Nobody volunteers any information except you. I suppose the aquatic theme occurred to me because of Venice's connections with the sea. Who's offering the commission?'

'The Marine Insurance Company of the Serenissima,' he said slowly. 'Originally a Venetian concern but now the biggest insurers of sea-going vessels and fisheries in Italy. They're building new head offices in Rome. So far I haven't given much thought to competing, because we have plenty of work on hand and in any case the best designers are all booked solid. Look—on Monday I'll give you the basic requirements for the screen—size, décor it's to fit in with, and so on. Get it down on paper, in rough, this coming week. If it seems even a remote possibility I'll bring in Innocenzo and the draughtsmen.'

Things were moving too fast. 'Innocenzo?' she repeated uneasily. 'Why Innocenzo?'

The clear eyes met hers in bland surprise. 'I thought you two got along?'

She wriggled further back in her seat. 'Er—yes. We do. He's very friendly.'

'I'm glad to hear it. Innocenzo is, to be frank, something of a problem. He's the son of my father's second cousin, and as such is keen to become part of the company. He's bright, but has no flair for business, neither has he any feeling for the glass, or any skill in making it, despite lengthy training. He has no inner vision of it—do you know what I mean? But of course you do!' He waved a confirmatory hand, as if their minds were perfectly attuned, and at that moment she felt as if that were the case. She'd sensed an apartness in Innocenzo, a difference. Was this the reason for it?

'What he does have,' continued Benvenuto, 'is the ability to translate a design into a detailed scale model for the men to follow. On occasion that ability is invaluable, and that's why I say I'll bring him in if you come up with anything. I'd like you to look at the screens being assembled in the fittings shop, observe how they're linked together, and how the pieces are elliptical—flattened out rather than fully three-dimensional, and see——'

In her agitation Miranda interrupted him. 'But Mr dei Santi, I'm not a designer, you know—I'm not——'

'I know,' he said patiently. 'But I've seen your sketches. They have a certain freshness, an originality, that appeals to me. Or perhaps you're worried that this will interfere with your studies of sculpture? Do you not see that screens are just another aspect of free-formed sculpture?'

'Of course I see it. And I'm not at all worried that it will interfere with anything else. It's just that I might not be any good at something so complicated . . . Still, it will make me feel I'm earning my wages.'

'Earning your wages?' He sounded as if that was the last thing he expected her to do. 'If you never so much as lift a hand in my glasshouse I don't think I'll go bankrupt because of the pittance I pay you, Miranda.'

'But you told me you don't run a philanthropic institution,' she said stubbornly. 'Surely that means you expect value for money?'

'Don't quibble,' he said dismissively, and strode to the door. 'Come along, we have just ten minutes left to look round the showrooms.' He picked up her jacket and wellingtons. 'You won't need these for much longer. The high tides are almost at an end, and the weather will soon get warmer.'

As they went down the stairs he said, 'I regret all this haste, but I'm catching the 12.30 train to Verona to go and see my new nephew. Four days old—he's my youngest sister's first child and my father's first grandson.'

Miranda beamed. She loved babies. 'What is he to be called?'

'Paolo after his father, Alessandro after his grandfather, Gabriele after me, and Sante by family tradition. Paolo Alessandro Gabriele Sante Molinari.' He looked down at her and raised one black eyebrow. 'And I'm Ben!'

'Yes, Ben,' she said, and with a laugh that was partly a sigh, followed him into the showroom.

She walked quietly round the displays, the man behind her commenting only rarely. 'We first made this line in 1800 ... this ruby and gold ware is popular, but perhaps a little ornate for your taste? ... These chandeliers—what do you think of the colours? ...'

Eyes huge with interest, jaw set in concentration, Miranda moved on rapidly. Ten minutes wasn't long ... She caught Benvenuto watching her and detected a faint smile. For goodness' sake—what was funny?

They moved on to modern glass. It was plain, stylish,

superb; the coloured pieces brilliant without ever being garish. It was the best she'd seen in Venice, and at once she told him so.

He didn't shrug modestly, or attempt to deny it. He merely nodded. 'Some of it is the best in Venice,' he agreed, 'but not all.'

'And where is your own work, Maestro?' Just in time she'd remembered that 'Ben' wasn't for use in front of the men, and the grey-haired salesman was hovering nearby.

The dark eyelashes flickered, showing he'd noticed the title, then he gestured towards a separate area by the windows. 'We have only seven pieces in stock just now. More will be brought across from the works tomorrow.'

The sulptures were uncoloured, crystal-clear, shining in the bright morning light. There were several abstract shapes, a magnificent winged lion, and a stylised impression of two little girls holding hands. There came upon Miranda a small ache in the region of her heart. It was an emotional thing, something she often experienced when she saw really beautiful glass.

Each piece was on its own matt black base, engraved with a facsimile signature in silver: *Benvenuto dei Santi*. The winged lion, though, bore only the surname. 'Why is this?' she asked, tracing the silver letters with a forefinger.

'The lion is a replica of my original, and made by Armani's men. Only my original pieces bear my full name.' He looked at his watch. 'Come and see our display of old glass.'

The dei Santi heirlooms were displayed in a showcase, and at once Miranda's attention was caught by the central exhibit—a dark green glass chalice decorated with enamelled garlands in white and gold, and with the dei Santi crest on one side and a man and woman in medieval dress on the other. The date was 1495.

'But this is only a little later than the Barovier *Coppa Nuziale*,' she said in awe, 'and that's the most celebrated piece of glass in Venice, isn't it? Is this—is it *yours*?'

'Yes.' He touched the rim of the chalice with long, gentle fingers. 'Yes, this is the dei Santi Marriage cup, used only on the marriage of a dei Santi son. The last time was when my father married my mother.' He left unsaid who was next in line, but the question was plain in Miranda's eyes.

'Yes, I'm next,' he said lightly, 'and taking far too long in reaching the altar, according to my family.' He lifted a shoulder and put out an upturned palm. 'But I haven't yet proposed to the lady, much less been accepted.'

Miranda looked away. Why tell her that? It was none of her business. But he went on, 'How about you, Miranda? Do you have a husband in mind at home?'

'No,' she said flatly. 'I shan't get married for ages. I want to establish myself in glass-making first.'

He seemed to have forgotten he was in a hurry, and stood leaning against the showcase, while at his side the glass chalice glowed like an emerald. 'What do you intend to do after your degree?' he asked.

'I don't know yet,' she admitted, 'but I'd like to spend a year gaining experience, then maybe apply to the Royal College of Art.'

'And after that?'

'Perhaps, one day, my own studio.' She shifted her feet restlessly, unsure why she felt so reluctant to discuss her future with him. She hurriedly changed the subject. 'Oh—are these old company accounts?'

'Yes. From 1700. And here's a chemical anlysis of the old 'Smeraldo' glass. As for the two goblets here, they were made in——'

He broke off as the staccato sound of a boat's horn came from the stone landing-stage outside the window. Swaying at the gold-painted posts was the dei Santi launch, with Baldassare at the controls.

Ben went to open the tall glass door, and in walked a slender, copper-haired figure. She put one hand to Ben's face and reached up to kiss him lightly on the mouth. Ben seemed unsurprised at the greeting. 'Elena,' he said, 'come and meet Miranda. You remember I told you all about her?'

He spared them the usual lengthy recital. All he said was, 'Miranda Brown of Stourley, England—Elena Comino, a friend of the family.'

A phrase echoed through Miranda's mind: 'I haven't yet proposed to the lady' . . . This, presumably, was the lady in question. It was somehow a surprise to find that she rather liked the look of her; the warm smile, the direct glance of intelligent brown eyes, the creamy skin. Not too young, either, thought Miranda; perhaps the same age as Ben . . . and as for the clothes . . . Colours to put off most redheads—a lilac cowl-necked dress topped by a throw in deep purple. On Elena they looked supremely elegant and slightly theatrical.

'So you're Miranda! What a surprise!' There was genuine interest in the long-lashed eyes. 'Ben, you horror—how could you—she's too pretty to be buried in that grubby hole on Murano!'

Miranda gaped. Ben a horror? And his glorious glasshouse a grubby hole? But he seemed unperturbed. 'That's what I thought,' he agreed mildly, 'but Miranda seems to like it.'

'I do,' she said quickly. 'I'm used to the glass industry.'

'Elena occupies herself with more glamorous pursuits,' Ben explained. 'She organises exhibitions and concerts, helps with the *Biennale*, and is already preparing for the Film Festival.'

Elena laughed. 'It's mad, absolutely hectic. You must come to one of my parties, Miranda, and meet some of the stars. I live across on the Lido only a hundred metres or so from the Palazzo del Cinema, so I give lots of parties during the Film Festival. Will you still be here in September?'

'I'm not sure yet.' Miranda darted a glance at her employer, but he gave neither confirmation nor denial.

'We must go, I'm afraid,' he said. 'Perhaps we can finish looking at the old pieces some other time, Miranda—or——' he gestured to the grey-haired salesman, 'Giuseppe can tell you anything you want to know ... Elena, let's be off.' At the door he turned, 'Miranda, how will you spend your day?'

'Exploring, I expect, and writing letters home.'

'Not out with your five friends, then?'

'We might go out later,' she conceded, 'and there are nine of us, not just five.'

He made no reply to that, but merely held the door for Elena, bent his head in farewell to Miranda, and went out to the launch. Elena turned to wave goodbye as she stepped aboard, and behind her Baldassare smiled and touched his peaked cap before starting the vessel on its journey to the station.

Miranda turned and found Giuseppe waiting to show her the rest of the exhibits but for some reason she didn't want anyone other than Ben to show her his family treasures. 'Perhaps some other time, thank you, Signor.'

Once outside, she headed for the Zattere quayside, her mind busily registering the morning's events, and her imagination providing an all too clear picture of a marriage where the dei Santi wedding cup would once again be put to use.

CHAPTER SEVEN

'*Buon giorno*, Miranda.' Innocenzo joined her as she walked in through the works gates. He was wearing one of his ultra-modern shirts and his most dazzling smile.

'Good morning, Innocenzo,' she said in English. 'Have you enjoyed the weekend?'

'*Prego?*'

'I was so pleased to hear that you speak excellent English. Perhaps you were under the impression that I must use only Italian?'

For once Innocenzo's un-innocent eyes evaded hers. 'The Maestro?' he asked awkwardly, 'he has told you of this?'

'No,' she said quietly. 'I haven't bothered the Maestro with it—yet. It was someone else who mentioned it. I just wanted to say how pleased I will be to call on your English when things are too complicated for me to understand.'

At any other time his expression would have amused her. Annoyance, tinged with alarm, overlaid by peevish ill-humour. Innocenzo Paulucci was not pleased, but he dredged up his smile again. 'It was a misunderstanding on my part, Miranda. A thousand apologies! Do you wish English or Italian between us in future?'

'Italian, I think. Unless I'm in difficulties. If that happens, perhaps you'll be good enough to translate?'

'Of course,' he agreed, and caught hold of her hand. He lifted it and kissed the inside of her wrist, as he did at least once a day. 'Perhaps I'll see you later, in the works?'

'Perhaps. I may be there before lunch. I'll be busy

94

with the Maestro for most of the afternoon.' That round to me, she thought emptily, as she walked through the offices and made for the stairs.

On her work-bench she found details of the requirements for the screen. It was to be huge, she saw, suitable for illuminating from behind, and would be situated in the foyer of a modern building nearing completion in Rome. The surrounding décor—walls, flooring, furnishings—was to be based on the focal point—namely, the screen. What a task!

By mid-morning she was at the easel finishing a colour-wash over a line sketch. It was only preliminary stuff; she was no designer, still less a draughtswoman, but she had the ability to express her ideas, and she knew exactly what she hoped to create. Later she would visit the fittings shop to examine the screens there to find out how they were linked and supported. And for that, she thought defiantly, she would use her notebook, whether the men liked it or not.

The phone rang. 'Miranda?' It was Ben dei Santi, brisk and business-like. 'Would it help you to have on hand our full range of colours in the grade of glass suitable for screens?'

'Yes,' she said eagerly. 'Yes, it would, Mr dei Santi.' She found herself staring at the receiver in amazement. Could the man read her mind as well as her eyes?

'Right. I'll have the samples from the lab sent up to you shortly. And I'll see you at one. Shall we use your studio or mine?'

Miranda gazed fondly round her room. 'Mine, please.'

He was in there, waiting, when she got back from her lunch-hour walk. 'Oh! I'm not late, am I?'

'No. I'm early. You've been out?'

'Yes. Exploring. It seemed mad to work on Murano

yet see nothing of the island, so I've decided to go out each lunchtime with a picnic snack.' She took her jacket to the washroom, and when she returned he was already in front of the easel. 'It's just a preliminary sketch,' she said defensively. 'A rough impression.'

He studied it minutely. 'It's certainly different. Have you started from scratch this morning?'

'No. I did the first rough drafts after I left you yesterday. The light in my room at the Signora's isn't good enough to do much in the evenings.'

'You're keen on the idea, then?'

'I want to have a go,' she said simply. 'If I don't ever attempt the difficult, or even the impossible, how will I ever improve? Oh, and may I come in late one morning so that I can visit the fish market? I thought I'd get some ideas from there.'

'Of course you can,' he sounded irritable. 'You're not on set hours, you know. Remember though, that the technical problems involved in making the screen will increase in direct proportion to the variety of its parts.'

'I'll remember. I see from the specification that it's to have a modern setting.'

'And you're pleased about that?'

'Yes,' she said simply. She knelt down by the trays of coloured samples, and picked up a piece in each hand. 'These colours are terrific, Mr dei Santi. All the shades I envisaged are here, except perhaps, a really dark, blackish green for some of the seaweed.'

Each labelled with its formula, the cubes of glass gleamed and glinted on the floor between them. Suddenly Ben knelt opposite her and placed his hands under hers, taking the weight of the pieces she was holding. 'When are you going to stop using "Mr dei Santi"?' he asked gently.

'I might manage to call you Ben,' she said impulsively, 'but I always think of you as Benvenuto.'

He seemed highly amused. 'Do you indeed? You see me as being more Italian than American, then?'

'More Venetian,' she said thoughtfully. 'Somehow, I don't think Venetians are typically Italian.'

'Very perceptive,' he said, replacing the glass back in the tray. 'One last point, Miranda, before we start work. My father is anxious to meet you.'

Her eyes widened. 'He's Alessandro dei Santi, isn't he?'

'The same,' he agreed.

'And—he's in Verona?'

'Yes. I hesitate to ask this, but could you manage next Sunday? It's the only day I'm free. I'll take you, of course.'

She couldn't prevent herself beaming in delight. Alessandro dei Santi, a legend in glassmaking, wanted to meet *her*, Miranda Brown of Stourley. 'I'd like that very much indeed. How was baby Paolo?'

'Noisy, red and wrinkled,' he said fondly. 'A fine boy.' Then, as if realising they were still on their knees, he jumped up. 'Come along. Get out your note book and we'll start work.' His warm hand gripped hers as he helped her up, then he went to the table by the window and pulled out two chairs. She glanced at her watch, and wasn't at all surprised to see that it was one o'clock to the very second.

That was the start of the busiest week of Miranda's entire life. The three-hour sessions she'd half-dreaded flew past like lightning. She learned so much in such a short time she became convinced that Ben was working at top speed in order to have a clear conscience about sending her home at the end of the trial period.

On that first day she'd arrived back at the Signora's to find extra power points installed in her room and a couple of Anglepoise lamps on the table. 'The

Maestro's orders,' declared the Signora, flashing her teeth, 'and all at his expense. He explained to me on the telephone that you need strong light for your work.'

'That's true,' agreed Miranda, 'how kind.' And how convenient, because she hoped to work in the evenings for the rest of the week.

She'd been relieved to find that their glass-making sessions took place on number six furnace, cut off from the others by the small partition there. Ben was a good teacher, with a vast store of patience, and he switched to English whenever he thought it would be easier for her. 'No . . . Handle your rod so . . . Look, it will be better like this . . . Only a very soft breath, hardly more than a sigh . . . Good . . . Excellent . . . Awful, try again . . . Lovely. Miranda, you're doing very well indeed! Now—you see how I handle it to put in more curve? We want this little dolphin to leap, don't we . . .?

At the end of that first session she had free-formed a little fish, supposedly a dolphin. Red-cheeked, hot and triumphant, she stood in front of the marver and watched her creation lose its glow and assume its own silver-grey colouring. Her heart was thudding. It made her tense to have Ben close enough to place his hands over hers on the rod.

He stood at her side, relatively cool and unruffled, his checked shirt still buttoned almost to the neck. 'That's good for your first attempt at free-forming, Miranda. You're a natural at handling the glass. The men will be impressed.'

'But they haven't seen me make it,' she pointed out, removing her denim cap.

'Oh, I think they have,' he said drily. 'The partition here makes you feel cut off, but you can take it from me that at least one of them has been watching from somewhere or other. There's no need to look upset, you'll have given them something to think about. Come along, let's go and have our session in the lab with Enrico.'

And that was how the week progressed. The mornings a whirl of drawing and painting, with reluctant forays into the works; the afternoons taken up with theory, spells in the lab and with the magical glass-making lessons in the glare of the furnace with Ben. Then in the evenings she worked again on her drawings, sometimes with Spiro or Danielle studying at her table.

The only light relief was an early morning visit to the *Pescheria*, the incomparable fish market of Venice, where she spent a happy couple of hours sketching the shapes, colours and textures of the infinite variety of fish on sale. Then, mindful of Ben's irritable reminder that she wasn't on set hours, she left the area of the Rialto and headed briskly for the Accademia Gallery.

At that time of day it was fairly quiet, and she was able to view some of the world's most celebrated paintings without distraction. She paid homage to Veronese's *Feast in the House of Levi*, admired masterpieces which were familiar from her studies of the Venetian painters, and observed with keen interest that Bellini had used the same model for several of his Madonnas; a serene young woman with a cast of features that looked very much at home in the twentieth century.

She allowed herself only an hour there before setting off on the ultimate time-consumer—the long, tortuous walk through the streets and alleys to the distant Fondamente Nuove and the *vaporetto* for Murano.

Miranda walked across the yard to the tower, feeling close to angry tears. It was some days later and she'd been in the fittings shop, where the men had done everything they could to show her she wasn't welcome there. Even Innocenzo, close by, hadn't prevented them jostling her and pretending she was in the way.

Her phone rang as she was making a pot of strong coffee to restore her morale. Despondently she lifted the receiver. *'Pronto?'*

'Miranda—can you spare a moment to come down to my office?'

The coffee would have to wait. She went down and Felicetta ushered her into the big square room. Ben dei Santi flicked a hand at his secretary. 'Right, Felicetta. No interruptions for ten minutes, if you please.' He gestured to one of the leather chairs. 'Sit down, Miranda.'

For once he was in formal business clothes, and she recalled that he'd had an early visit from an export customer. He leaned forward with his hands flat on the desk and went straight to the point. 'I've just had an official complaint about you from the fittings shop. They say you were in the way on the shop floor, and that your presence there prevented the men from doing their work.'

'Oh yes?' She wasn't exactly surprised about that, and her tone said as much.

He tilted his chair back and watched her keenly, his eyes narrowed. 'I've told them I'll speak to you about it, but naturally I want to hear what you have to say about it. Did you accidentally get in the way of the men?'

'No,' she said shortly, 'I didn't *accidentally* get in their way—I didn't get in their way *at all*. Why not ask Innocenzo? He was there.'

'It was Innocenzo who delivered the complaint,' said Ben soberly. 'And it won't help me in the least if you're aggressive about it.'

'I was not in anyone's way,' she insisted. 'I know they hate having me around—do you think I'd be such a fool as to give them the perfect excuse to get rid of me? I was standing to one side, and that big fellow with the bull neck jostled me and then his bit-boy came forward and blocked my path.' She stopped, dismayed to hear her voice trembling.

He looked furious. 'You're sure of that?'

'Yes,' she said wearily, 'of course I am. Why would I risk giving them cause for a genuine complaint?' She gripped the edge of the desk with both hands. 'Mr dei Santi—I don't know if I can go on with this—forcing my presence on them when they don't want me. I feel terrible when I have to go into the works. It needs someone with the hide of a rhinoceros. I don't think I'm soft, but I'm afraid I'm not all that hard, either.'

He watched her, his eyes still glittering with anger. 'You do realise that I can't afford a show-down? I can't risk any of my best men leaving me—they'd be snapped up at once by the other houses on Murano.'

'Of course I realise it!' She jumped up, suddenly enraged. 'And you realised it when you asked me to come here—you must have done! You knew then there'd be trouble. Answer me this, Ben dei Santi: did you bring me here because you liked my work or to demonstrate to everyone that dei Santi is progressive, training a foreigner, and a woman at that!'

She glared at him across the desk, her lips jutting ominously. 'Well?' she demanded. 'Did you bring me here to make your point?'

He stared at her, his eyes unreadable. 'Yes, I did,' he admitted quietly.

'Oh!' She felt sick, so she sank down on the chair again. 'And—and that's why you were amazed when you saw I wasn't an old campaigner who could handle all the aggro?'

'It wasn't so much your youth and lack of experience as a certain—vulnerability—that made me doubt whether you could handle all the aggro, as you put it.'

She jumped up again. 'Well—now you have the

answer—I can't! I simply can not keep going into the
works as if I'm so thick I believe they're all delighted to
see me. I can't do it. And—and another thing—it's
going to damage your relations with the men . . .' She
sat down again and stared at her fingers.

'Oh, sit *still*, Miranda. You're up and down like a
jack-in-the-box.' He pressed the switch of the intercom.
'Felicetta—get Paulucci here at once, if you please.
Miranda—when he comes don't speak unless I address
you directly. As for my relationship with my men, let
me worry about that. I have no intention of sacrificing
all my principles in order to keep them working for me.
But it's not so simple as it appears. They aren't really
heartless and unkind, just bound up in tradition and
very touchy about it. They're creative artists, each with
his share of the artistic temperament.'

They both fell silent, Miranda appalled at what she'd
asked, and even more so at the answer she'd been given.
She felt sure that in minutes she was going to get her
marching orders, and amazingly, she felt nothing but
relief. All at once life in Stourley seemed safe and secure
and very much to be desired.

She decided to save him the trouble of firing her, and
stood up again. 'I'm ready to go home right now,' she
announced belligerently. 'I don't want to wait until the
month's up!' At that moment Innocenzo came in, out of
breath and unmistakably wary.

Ben ignored what she'd said, and turned to the other
man. 'Ah, Innocenzo. Miranda tells me that you can
back up her claim that she wasn't hindering the men in
their work. What do you say to that?'

The beautiful, intelligent eyes flicked from Ben to her
and back again. She noted that he didn't answer the
question directly. 'I've just been speaking to the men,
Maestro. They don't wish any unpleasantness, you
understand. I think that after discussion they will

withdraw the complaint.'

'I see. It was somewhat premature, then?'

Innocenzo looked modestly at his feet. 'They now believe so.'

'Mm. Did you yourself see any cause for complaint?'

An expression of troubled frankness came over the perfect features. 'Perhaps Miranda was a little too close to Lorenzo ... but nothing to merit an official complaint, Maestro.'

'Thank you. It seems you've averted an open confrontation, but we don't want to risk more trouble. Miranda—how would it suit you to have Innocenzo escort you whenever you enter the works?'

She almost missed the flash of resentment in Innocenzo's eyes. It wasn't to be wondered at, she thought. He believed himself to be above acting as watchdog to a female student ... 'I don't think so, Maestro,' she said carefully. 'I feel it would put Innocenzo at a disadvantage. At present he is impartial. Give him me to watch over, and by implication, he's on my side. No—I'll be better on my own—if I stay.'

She sensed relief in Innocenzo's slim figure. 'Perhaps Miranda is right, Maestro. Let us see how next week progresses.'

'Very well. That's all for now, then. Thank you.'

The younger man bent his head respectfully and left with a wide smile in Miranda's direction. Once through the door, imagining Ben couldn't see him, he actually blew her a kiss.

'At least Innocenzo supports you,' said Ben, eyebrows raised.

She made no reply. If that was how he saw it, who was she to disillusion him? He came round to her side of the desk and stook looking down at her. 'All this talk of leaving. Are you serious, Miranda?'

She had calmed down a little by then. 'I don't know,' she admitted.

'Are you not happy here?'

'I'm happy to be having personal tuition from you,' she said carefully. 'I realise I'm fortunate in that, but I'm not at all happy at being brought here as a defiant gesture against the Venetian establishment, even though for some time I've suspected that to be the case.'

'Have you indeed?' He sat on the edge of the desk, drumming his fingers on its surface. 'Well, your suspicions are now confirmed. I deeply regret having distressed you, but you asked me and I told you the truth. I try not to hedge when I'm asked a direct question. The fact remains that I very much liked the baby's head. I could see in it a great potential—an untapped talent—and I wanted that talent here at dei Santi's. I still do.'

She looked up at him, her mind still on its separate track. 'On my first morning here you told me to trust you,' she said.

'So? Nothing has changed. You can still trust me. Do you doubt it?'

Her lips moved in the semblance of a smile. 'May I go now?'

'No. Not until I know what you've decided. Are you going to stay?'

'Oh—I'll stay,' she said listlessly. 'Until the next incident. Then I suppose we'll go through this whole performance again. I hope you find I'm worth all the bother.' Without another glance in his direction she left the office. A moment later she left the works. It seemed to her that an extra-long lunch hour was called for.

It was very quiet on the cemetery island. Sheer impulse had brought her; she'd seen a *vaporetto* starting its return journey and had hurried aboard, alighting when

it made its obligatory stop at San Michele. She needed
solitude and tranquillity in which to assess the events of
the past two weeks, and a sombre setting seemed right
for her mood.

To her surprise she found that the little island wasn't
sombre at all. There was an air of quiet, matter-of-fact
reverence, but no gloom, no despair, and the
atmosphere acted like balm on her overstrung nerves.
Two elderly ladies passed by, carrying flowers; a burly
gardener was bedding out plants behind a hedge, and in
the distance she could see a priest walking back and
forth beneath the high, white-banded walls.

She could smell narcissi as she sat on the steps of a
curved memorial wall. The midday sun poured down,
giving a foretaste of the coming summer, and there was
no sound to be heard except the gardener's trowel
piercing the soil, the murmuring of the two old ladies,
and the timeless slapping of the water beyond the walls.

She sat in the sun until the tensions and frustrations
of the glasshouse receded. It wasn't just the hostility of
the men, it was Ben's motivation in bringing her to
Venice that really hurt. All those tremors of doubt,
those twinges of unease—they'd all been justified.

Miranda thought of the look on his face as he made
the admission—no self-justification, no half-truths, no
excuses, just a stony-faced admission that he'd brought
her here to prove his point. Again she felt that odd
sensation within her chest, as if her heart had changed
position ... She passed her fingers up and down her
breast-bone and leaned wearily against the warm stone.

Until now she had imagined that her emotions had
been heightened because she was working with a world-
famous artist in glass, who also happened to be a
forceful and very attractive man. She breathed the scent
of the narcissi and told herself that she would never
again smell spring flowers without thinking of

Benvenuto dei Santi. Heaven help her, she'd fallen in love with him—the man who had manipulated her arrival in Venice as a means of proving his liberal and progressive views on employing foreigners.

Was she completely mad? It was barely a week since he'd looked at the dei Santi marriage cup and said, 'I haven't yet proposed to the lady', and a moment later had sailed off with Elena Comino to visit his family ... Miranda closed her eyes to shut out the picture of Elena with her hand to Ben's face, kissing his lips ... The cypresses swayed above her, their spires dark against the sky. It was very quiet and very warm ...

It seemed only a moment before a warm hand touched hers. 'Miranda?' She opened her eyes to see crystal-clear grey ones only inches away. Half asleep, still bemused by the discovery that she loved him, she breathed his name. 'Benvenuto ...'

For the space of a second she felt it only natural that he would kiss her. His eyes seemed dark and smoky and he leaned even closer. Then she remembered why she was there, and sat up abruptly, pushing him to one side. She felt stiff and her back hurt where it had been pressed against the stone wall. 'I fell asleep,' she said unnecessarily. 'What time is it? What are you doing here?'

'It's three o'clock, and I'm here because I've been looking for you and so has Baldassare. We rang the Signora and searched all Murano, and then I thought you might possibly be here. I was—worried, Miranda.'

She stared at him without speaking. She'd walked out of the works in a temper and he'd been worried. Worried enough to search for her. She moistened her lips. Of course—didn't he keep on telling her that he felt responsible for her?

'I want to apologise,' he said evenly. 'I now realise more clearly than ever that I've been unfair to you.' He moved his shoulders uncomfortably. 'I ask for your forgiveness.'

She knew he was speaking words that did not come easily. He was finding it difficult to apologise. Looking at his face now, she was absolutely certain that she could trust him, no matter what had been his motives in bringing her here. She loved him. She smiled the wide, sweet smile of her generous, warm-hearted nature. 'There's nothing to forgive,' she said simply. 'I'm sorry too. Sorry for that awful display of temperament and pique. I was a bit worked up, you see.'

He pulled her to her feet. Then he turned her hand over and looked at the palm. There was a smear of sea-green paint on it. He bent, put his lips right on the smear, and kissed it. She felt her hand tremble and stiffened her fingers to still them, knowing that she would have given anything for him to take her in his arms. He was hesitating, with his mouth close to the soft flesh of her upper arm. Could he know what she was thinking? She lowered her eyes—hadn't he said that they were easy to read?

When he spoke his words seemed stilted. 'Shall I take you home or do you want to go back to see the racing yacht come out of the lehr?'

'Go back, please,' she said quietly.

They walked side by side through the arched gateway to the paved area in front of the little church of San Michele. He helped her aboard the launch and then turned it towards Murano. Minutes later they stopped at the water-gate of the works, closely followed by Baldassare in one of the work boats.

'Ho there, Maestro! You have found little Mee-ran-dah?'

'I've found her, Baldassare, safe and sound.'

With a flash of the dazzling smile Ben leapt up the steps ahead of her and opened the gate. He held it wide as she passed through.

'Welcome back,' he said quietly in her ear.

CHAPTER EIGHT

THERE were twenty or more students gathered by the railings around the bronze statue of a horseman in the Campo San Zanipolo. It was an international gathering, with Miranda the only English person there.

They all chatted together, drank coke or cheap wine from the *trattoria* alongside, and listened to guitars. Above them the most famous horseback figure in the world stared imperiously into the distance, but the noisy group weren't concerned with Colleone, dead for five hundred years; it was Saturday night and they were out with their friends.

Everything was relaxed and lighthearted, and Miranda found herself comparing the atmosphere with the tension and stress she'd experienced in the last two weeks. She had found that being in love with the boss did nothing at all to help her come to terms with the animosity of his work-force. Come to that, it didn't do much for her, either, except fill her with doubts about her own sanity.

'More wine, Miranda?' She allowed Spiro to fill up her glass and as usual, he carried on talking, his fractured Italian understandable now beneath the strong Greek accent. Although it was after nine, she was still warm enough in her cotton skirt and top. If it was as mild as this in May, what would it be like in high summer, she wondered, as she sipped her wine and Spiro murmured amorously at her side.

Danielle was the first to notice the man watching them from the shadows of the great church. 'Miranda,' she hissed, 'isn't that your Mr dei Santi over there?'

Even as she spoke Ben moved towards them, the
lamplight catching the glint of his remarkable eyes.

Spiro had drunk a lot of wine, and on seeing the
older man's approach he pulled Miranda towards him
and attempted to fill up her glass. 'It is the weekend,' he
declared loudly. 'You don't have to work *all* the time,
Miranda.'

She shrugged him away and turned to greet Ben. It
was so good to see him she had to force herself to speak
like a polite employee, and the words came out
abruptly. 'Hello. Do you want to see me?'

The noise went on around them. Someone was
singing, the guitars were playing, glasses were clinking
and everyone was talking at once. 'I tried to telephone
you, Miranda, but the Signora said you were out with
the others, and likely to be here.'

She waited. He eyed the crowd curiously, then
nodded to Danielle and put one hand against the
railings next to Miranda and effectively sealed her off
from the others. 'I wondered if your drawings are
sufficiently advanced to take to Verona tomorrow? My
father is something of an expert on screens and could
give us his opinion.'

Miranda's heart plummeted. She wasn't at all sure
that she wanted her efforts examined by an expert, least
of all the legendary Alessandro. 'You can have a look
at them now, to see what you think,' she offered
reluctantly.

'But what about your friends?'

'Oh—they can manage without me. Spiro ...
Danielle ... I'm going back to the house for a while.'
Ignoring Spiro's furious glare she went with Ben to the
dark waterway which led straight back to Due Ponti,
where he halted the launch between the two little
bridges.

Signora Gaspari appeared on the landing as they

climbed the stairs. 'Ah, it is you, Maestro.' Reassured, she flashed them a toothy smile and went back to her television.

Once in her room Miranda lit the lamps and whipped away a lacy bra and pants that were drying on her towel rail. Quickly she spread her sketches on the table, seeing with dismay that what had earlier seemed so fresh and original now looked, with Ben there, like amateurish daubs. Hastily she took out her more detailed drawings and laid them on the bed.

He examined them, one by one. 'But what is this?' he asked suddenly. On Miranda's pillow lay a Greek textbook on stone restoration.

'That? Oh, it's Spiro's.' She turned back to her work. 'This drawing shows the sea creatures in——'

'The Greek comes in here?' There was an edge to his voice that she didn't much care for. Obviously he was back in his role of watchdog against 'the dregs of Europe'.

'Yes,' she said lightly. 'Often. And so does Danielle.' She held up a sheaf of notes in the French girl's sprawling hand. 'But the Signora ensures that no scenes of debauchery take place. She has a house rule that doors must be left open when we're in each other's rooms. If it wasn't for that anything might happen.'

'Don't be flippant,' he said shortly. 'Might I ask why they should study in here?'

She concealed a smile. 'Because the light is so much better.'

That silenced him, and not surprisingly, since he was responsible for the improved lighting. He continued to examine the drawings, each sheet of which highlighted a different aspect of the screen. 'These are remarkably accomplished, Miranda. You've worked hard—well done. We'll take them with us tomorrow. I'll pick you up about ten, if that's convenient?'

'Yes, that's fine.'

'We'll have lunch with my family, and a session with my father; then if you like I'll show you round Verona.' Miranda's eyes were dark in the lamplight, but he looked into them and said with remarkable insight, 'Yes, we'll go and see Juliet's balcony.'

She stared, dumbfounded. How could he possibly have known she was longing to see it? He turned to go. 'Until tomorrow, then?'

Miranda was more than ready for an early night, but she couldn't let him have everything his own way, even if she *had* fallen for him. 'Just a moment. Perhaps you'll drop me off at San Zanipolo on your way back?'

He looked amazed. 'You're going back? Now?'

'Oh yes,' she said calmly. 'After all, this is my first free evening all week.'

Silently he held open the door. A quick glance at his face showed that he'd got the message. Outside the glasshouse she was her own woman, and did what she pleased.

The launch arrived at ten, with Ben at the controls and next to him Baldassare in his Sunday-best suit. Miranda had gone to some trouble with her appearance; her hair newly washed and with Danielle's help subdued to a mass of shining waves, a light film of make-up on her perfect skin, and subtle shadowing emphasising her enormous eyes. She looked what she was—a pretty fair-skinned English girl with a magnificent mane of hair. She'd put on pink strappy sandals and carried her pink leather bag, and for the first time wore a mist-grey lacy-knit dress bought in Birmingham with money from her great-uncle Matthew.

As Ben helped her aboard he said quietly, 'Miranda, you look beautiful.'

Her heart sang. Ben thought she was beautiful. The

sun seemed brighter, the sky more blue. She resolved to
stop agonising about being in love with someone
unattainable, and to enjoy this one day when she was to
meet his family and be with him all the time.

They left Baldassare and zoomed out of the city in a
two-seater Lamborghini, which she knew would have
sent her brothers into ecstasies. 'The car? Oh—I've
hired it,' said Ben. 'I don't even own one—they're
superfluous in Venice. In fact, Venetians are reputed to
be the world's worst drivers, did you know that? If I
want to travel by road then I hire.'

She sat contentedly at his side as they joined the
autostrada, watching the lean, confident hands on the
wheel and trying to ignore the noise and smell of the
traffic, which seemed overpowering after her time in a
city devoid of wheeled transport.

There was something about Sunday lunch at the dei
Santi villa that reminded Miranda of a family meal at
home in Stourley. It wasn't the setting; the big, cream-
washed house in its terraced gardens overlooking
Verona was quite unlike the Browns' small, detached
home above its Midlands river.

Then, different again, servants were on hand to serve
the dei Santi meal; *fettucine* with spicy tomato sauce,
chicken breasts stuffed with herbs and peppers and a
large exotic salad, a layered coffee meringue and what
seemed to Miranda to be vast quantities of the local
Soave wine. At home it would probably be the
traditional Sunday roast with baked potatoes and two
veg, followed by one of Betty's delectable fruit pies and
perhaps a bottle of cider to please Seb and Dick, with a
cup of tea or coffee afterwards.

Nor could she see similarity in the two families. The
people around her were unmistakably Italian, with the
style and gloss of wealth. Alessandro was at the head of

the table, gaunt and unsmiling, with the same facial bone structure as his son and black, deep-set eyes. There was an elderly aunt, fragile but still elegant; Ben's sisters, Sophia and Francesca, and their husbands; Sophia's two little girls, shy and polite and exquisitely dressed, and finally baby Paolo, sleeping peacefully amid the noise of a talkative family.

Miranda sat there, eating unfamiliar food in the beautiful room with the spectacular view, wondering what it could be that was so like home. It came to her eventually. It was the atmosphere created by a loving family. And the way they treated her was how the Brown family would treat a foreigner in their midst, though perhaps the blunt good manners of the Black Country *were* a little unlike the graceful courtesies of Italy.

Yes, that was what reminded her of Stourley. Not the way everything looked, but the way everything *was*. She felt at home with the dei Santis. As a family they were very likeable, but it was Francesca who fascinated her. Still slightly plump from her pregnancy, and not much older than Miranda herself, she had an air of chic modernity allied to a sweetness and serenity that made Miranda think of Bellini's Madonnas at the Accademia. She found herself studying the new mother's every smile, every glance towards her baby, because she knew she was going to draw that face beneath its smooth dark hair just as soon as she could find an opportunity.

The little girls were excused from the table, and minutes later reappeared with evidence that the American influence still counted in the family—their embroidered dresses had been replaced by practical dungarees and tee shirts. After a whispered consultation with each other and a kiss for their grandpa they skipped outside to play in the garden.

And then the baby wakened. No sooner did he

squeak than his father scooped him up and cuddled him. Francesca left the table, declaring that Paolo was ready for his feed, and departed with husband and baby to another room.

Miranda felt edgy. She was anxious not to miss the chance of sketching the young mother and her baby, and hesitantly asked Ben what he thought of the idea. 'She'd love it,' he said, surprised. 'She'll bring Paolo back in here later. But first Father wants to talk to us about the screen.'

The three of them went some distance from the house to a working studio fitted out with glassmaking equipment, including a small, gas-fired furnace. Miranda spread out various sheets of her design, and as she stood at Alessandro's side could hear a faint but perceptible wheeze from his chest, evidence of the condition which had caused him to leave Venice and his glasshouse long before his creative skills were exhausted.

He pinned up the sheets one at a time on a wallboard, and prowled back and forth in front of them, his thin figure erect, his iron-grey hair flapping untidily when he turned. He shot questions at her, and she answered respectfully, addressing him as 'Maestro', and when she had time told herself that this was Alessandro dei Santi looking at her work!

'When do you take your final examinations, Signorina? Your main interest is in glass sculpture? Now, where are your measurements for this section? So? That is unusual . . .'

Miranda felt dazed by his quick-fire mixture of English and Italian, and acutely conscious of the silent, dark-haired figure watching them both with that glittering, all-seeing regard.

At last the older man announced that he would let them have his opinion on the feasibility of the screen by telephone the next morning. Miranda felt flattered. He was giving her ideas the same careful consideration as he would give to the work of a professional designer; and what was more she could detect no sign of prejudice against her because of either her sex or her nationality.

After that her time with Francesca and the baby was outwardly tranquil. They went to a small room facing the hills at the rear of the house, and Francesca sat there with a sleeping Paolo in her arms, looking from him to Miranda, who was crouching intently over her sketch book.

It was one of the times when pure artistic instinct swept her along. Having experienced violent creative impulses before, she knew it was pointless to question this sense of urgency, and so she let her pencil race through several swift sketches of the mother and baby.

Francesca took it all quite calmly, and in her pretty English remarked that already her husband had taken lots of photographs of her and baby Paolo, and that if Miranda wished it she would send her prints of some he had taken only that morning.

Smilingly accepting the offer, Miranda realised with a jolt that she could very easily become attached to the entire dei Santi family. Honestly—she'd let herself get too interested in Benvenuto and now she was all set to start doting on his family as well. For heaven's sake— she might never see any of them again.

It shook her somewhat to hear his name spoken out loud. 'Benvenuto, my brother,' said Francesca suddenly. 'You like?'

'Uh? Oh yes, I like,' admitted Miranda. And how, she added silently.

She looked up to find the dark, questioning eyes watching her intently. 'Do you not find it strange that a man such as he is not married, nor even betrothed?'

asked Francesca, apparently quite ready to discuss her
brother with his student-trainee.

Miranda hesitated. 'No, I don't find it strange. In
England we look at things a little differently than you
do here in Italy.'

'Ah yes, I forget. Here, the aunts and the uncles say it
is not fitting for the dei Santi son to remain unmarried,
but our father is not as other Italians. He does not—
how do you say——?'

'Conform?'

'Is that the word? I wish to say he does not always go
with tradition himself, and so he does not expect Ben to
do this, either.'

Miranda swallowed the question that trembled on her
lips. Was Ben not hoping to marry Elena, then?

'The women like my brother,' went on Francesca.
'Once upon a time we thought he would marry, but the
girl was drowned in the sea of the Venice Lido. It was a
matter of great tragedy, Miranda. All Verona mourned,
because two young men also died that night, the
brother of Elena Comino and the man she was to
marry. Elena is still single. Yes, to this day.'

'How awful!' The stab of pain she'd felt initially was
smothered by ready sympathy for Elena. To lose fiancé
and brother in the same accident . . .

The baby squirmed, and let out a wail. 'Oh, oh, his
little tummy!' said his mother, back in her native
tongue. She put him up to her shoulder and rubbed his
back.

Miranda closed her sketch book. 'I've finished now,
thanks, Francesca. Shall we go back?'

Francesca beamed as Paolo gave a little burp. 'If I
take your sketch book, you may carry Paolo.'

Accepting the honour eagerly, Miranda carried the
small, warm bundle to his carry-cot and thanked
Francesca again. What might have been a tranquil

interlude had left her feeling drained yet oddly reassured.

When it was time to leave, Alessandro held up a delaying hand and led them back to his studio. He went to his polishing bench and returned carrying a perfect sphere of glass, similar to a clairvoyant's crystal ball. Lifting Miranda's hands he kissed each palm, cupped them together, and on them placed the glass ball. 'This is for you,' he said, almost smiling. 'It is a new formula. Benvenuto knows I have been working on it.'

Somewhat overcome, Miranda thanked him; then, lips parted, the tip of her tongue protruding in concentration, she studied the glass. It was dazzlingly clear, but somewhere in the lustrous depths was a subtle tinge of gold. She carried it to the doorway, where sunlight slanted down beneath tall cypresses. The glass was unbelievably beautiful, and she felt the familiar tugging sensation round her heart. In that instant she knew without doubt what she would like to see made from it.

'Is this a glass suitable for sculpture, Maestro?'

'Assuredly.' He watched her with the intent expression that was also his son's, from the face that was uniquely his own.

'And does it have a name?' she asked.

'*Sì*. Dei Santi gold,' was the reply.

From that moment on Miranda began to imagine that everything in Verona was tinged with gold. The whole family came out to say goodbye; the little girls rained kisses on their uncle, and clad as they were in dungarees, dropped quaint little curtsies to Miranda.

Paolo was asleep, one tiny fist against his chin, his cheeks pink and a film of milk on his mouth. Ben took him gently from Francesca, and held him for a moment before dropping a kiss on the fuzz of dark hair. He

glanced up and found Miranda watching him, so she
looked elsewhere. There was something that disturbed
her in the sight of that powerful figure holding the
baby.

And then they were descending the hills in the
Lamborghini, while far below the River Adige looped
its way through the city, green-gold in the afternoon
sun. It was an effort to direct her thoughts back to
Alessandro, who after all had been the instigator of her
visit. 'Ben, what do you think was your father's reaction
to the screen?'

'He was impressed,' he said at once. 'If he hadn't
been he would have wasted no time on it, I can assure
you. But look—I want you to forget work for a while.
I'm going to give you a conducted tour of Verona,' he
glanced at his watch, 'and get you back to Venice by
early evening.'

Disappointment gripped her, hard, but she managed
a smile. He had never mentioned doing anything other
than showing her round Verona, so why should she
have imagined they might spend the evening together?
They drove across the wide, fast-flowing Adige into the
heart of the city, where he took her straight to the
Roman Arena and stopped the car. 'Can you walk in
those shoes?' he asked. 'It will be more interesting for
you on foot.'

Miranda wiggled her toes. 'Yes. Can we go inside
here?'

He took her inside the immense amphitheatre, still
used for open air performances of opera, and then
showed her old churches, crenellated castles, ancient
palaces and the house where Romeo was said to have
lived.

'And now,' he said gently, 'we'll go and see Juliet's
balcony.'

This time, forewarned, she didn't cry for her mother,

although the wary expression on Ben's face made her think he'd half-expected it. He took her beneath an arch leading from a busy street, and at once, with silent tact, moved away from her side, leaving her alone.

They were in a little courtyard, where trees dipped their branches above an old iron lamp and trailing plants tumbled new leaves over a high wall. Miranda stepped back and looked up. The house of the Capulets was very, very old. Set high in the front of it was an enclosed balcony made of wood, and to its left another one of iron . . . but beneath them both was a balcony of stone surmounting two arched windows—Juliet's balcony.

It was so unspoiled, so absolutely right, that she was enchanted. In imagination she could see the young Romeo standing on the same spot as herself, and the fourteen-year-old Juliet gazing down on him from the balcony. It was almost inevitable that she thought then about her mother, but this time there was no sadness; just a comforting memory of her, thoughtful and always loving, as if she had just walked through that courtyard of the Capulets.

She turned to Ben, but he was behind her, waiting by the wall. Eyes shining, she ran across to him. 'It's lovely!' she breathed. 'Lovely! Just what I hoped for, but didn't really expect.'

He looked down at her, his face in shadow. 'Did you imagine you might be disappointed?'

'Oh yes. You know what it's like when for ages you've looked forward to seeing something. Quite often the reality doesn't come up to your expectations.'

'As with your first sight of Venice?'

'Yes.' She thought back to that afternoon, and their subsequent ride down the Grand Canal. 'But thanks to you I wasn't disappointed for long.'

At that he smiled, and for an instant they faced each

other in the quiet courtyard, with Juliet's balcony above
them, and a faint breeze whispering through the leaves
of the trees. Then a group of tourists came in, their
guide already holding forth in rapid French, so
Miranda left him and walked round slowly, giving it a
last, all-encompassing look. Out in the street it dawned
on her that it was already late afternoon. 'Do you want
to set off back, Ben?'

'Not just yet.' He took her by the arm and led her
towards the river. They emerged on a high embankment
lined with trees and old houses. 'Here we are,' he said
suddenly, and stopped outside a quiet restaurant. She
was wondering what meals they were likely to serve at
that hour on a Sunday afternoon when Ben indicated a
sign in the doorway: English Afternoon Tea.

They sat by a window, eating tiny cucumber
sandwiches and sponge cake filled with fresh cream and
raspberry jam, and drinking several cups of excellent
tea. Miranda couldn't remember when she'd last had
afternoon tea. To her it conjured up old ladies wearing
hats in chintzy cafés, and a busy Midlands student had
little time for that sort of thing. But here, in this very
Italian city, the act of pouring tea from a silver pot and
eating traditional English food made her feel passionately, irrevocably English, and as if afternoon tea was
virtually the mainstay of her diet.

She felt distinctly odd. Ben's latest act of kindness in
bringing her here specially for afternoon tea seemed to
be having the effect of making her tearful. Then as she
drank a last cup of tea she started to wonder what they
were all doing at home, and felt a surge of longing for
Stourley. She put down her cup and stared at it intently.
Honestly—she was out for the day with the man she
loved, in this beautiful, beautiful city, and all she could
do was feel homesick.

'What's the matter, Miranda?'

'Nothing. I suppose it's just that I'm a bit overcome by all I've seen and done, that's all. Thank you for a lovely day. Verona is the second most beautiful city I've ever seen.'

'And which is the first?'

'Need you ask? Venice, of course.'

He smiled at that, and she felt the usual weird reaction. 'Tell me a little about your family,' he said suddenly.

It was exactly what she needed to ward off the pangs of homesickness. She told him about her father, with his quiet sense of humour and his garden and his work in the glass industry; about Seb training in electronics and Dick approaching his 'A' levels, and of little Bobby with his inexhaustible energy.

'And what of your stepmother?' Ben asked gently. 'I take it you don't resent her?'

'No. I'm fond of Betty, and I welcomed her marrying Dad for two reasons. One was purely practical, I'm afraid, in that she relieved me of a lot of housework and cooking. After Mum died I found it hard work, coping both at home and at college.'

She saw that he looked baffled, and wondered if he'd imagined she came from a wealthy family. 'Dad and the boys were good, of course, but we couldn't afford paid help in the house,' she said frankly. 'We're not well off, Ben. Far from it. The other reason I welcomed Betty was because I was sure she'd always been in love with my father.'

He was listening with close attention, as if nothing and no one else existed at that moment. 'Go on.'

'She'd always been a sort of family friend—the lady who worked in the baker's shop at the corner. She'd never married—never come near it, as far as I know, although she's attractive and extremely pleasant. There was just something in her eyes when he was around. I guessed how she felt about him when I was only fourteen or so, but Dad never really noticed her. Then, when at last he did finally pay attention to her, two years after Mum died, she agreed to marry him almost at once. How could I not be happy for both of them? In all those years she'd never wanted anyone else, you see.' Miranda stopped, and the colour rose in her cheeks. How she'd gone on! What had possessed her?

Ben's face was unreadable, which was perhaps as well. 'You value constancy in love, then?'

'Yes,' she said simply.

'And have you ever been in love, Miranda?'

She found herself resenting the question, so she avoided those all-too-observant eyes and wondered how he would react if she asked him about the girl who had drowned. 'No, just teenage crushes,' she said at last, and picked up her bag. 'I'm ready to go when you are.'

They went back through avenues of expensive shops. High heels clicking, the mist-grey dress swirling around her legs, she walked along with his impersonal hand beneath her arm. And that, she told herself bleakly, was the one sombre note in this beautiful, golden day. In spite of his kindness to her, his thoughtfulness, there wasn't even a hint of any deeper feeling.

She looked back over their brief acquaintance. He'd kissed her several times—on the hand; a salutation that in Italy meant little more than a handshake. She stole a sideways look at the lips which had kissed her palm. It was a firm, rather beautiful mouth above the dark-shadowed jaw, and she'd seen it warmed by that dazzling smile, pursed in thought, tight with concentration, teeth bared in irritation, and two days ago she'd seen it softened by the framing of an apology.

Perhaps one day he would ... No! She'd indulged herself already by imagining he was interested in her as a woman—an hour ago beneath Juliet's balcony, the time she awoke from sleep on San Michele, and the day they knelt by the samples of glass in her studio . . .

There, among Veronese families out for their Sunday promenade, Miranda felt gloom descend. It was typical of her, with her mile-wide streak of romanticism. She couldn't fall for one of the students at the college, nor indulge in a light flirtation with, say, Innocenzo, nor even fall for Spiro, likeable and clever and all agog to make love to an English blonde. Oh no. She had to go for a world-class artist who lived in the most romantic city on earth, who could trace back his family for five centuries, who was extremely wealthy, and who, moreover, was deeply involved with a beautiful woman of his own class and culture.

Being in love with such a man would bring her nothing but heartache. Well, she mustn't allow it to develop. It was as simple as that. She was in Italy to learn about glass, not to fall in love.

They passed the Arena and reached the car, and she was amazed at how exhausted she felt. As if sensing it, Ben drove her swiftly out of Verona, and she sat in silence as the powerful car sped along the *autostrada* called 'La Serenissima' beneath a sky streaked with flame and rose. They found Baldassare waiting for them at the Piazzale Roma, for all the world as if he hadn't moved since that morning.

Ben said quietly, 'I'll have to leave you now, Miranda. Baldassare is taking me home the quick way down the Giudecca. I have to change and get across to the Lido pretty quickly.'

He beckoned a water-taxi and put her aboard, handing her the parcel containing the sphere of gold-tinted glass. She clutched it and put her sketch book under her arm. 'What about my drawings of the screen?' she asked.

'I'll take them to the glasshouse for you in the

morning,' he said, then to the boatman, 'Due Ponti.' He paid him, and leaned down to Miranda. 'Until tomorrow.'

'Thanks again,' she said earnestly.

'Thank *you*, Miranda.'

The two boats moved off in different directions. She turned to see Baldassare still at the wheel, heading for the broad Giudecca canal, with Ben standing next to him, his hair glinting in the light of the lamps.

She leaned back wearily in her seat. No prizes for guessing whom he was in such a hurry to see across at the Lido!

CHAPTER NINE

BY nine a.m. on Monday Alessandro had telephoned his approval of the screen, qualified by various suggestions and warnings. Ben had told her the news in the tower room. 'I've given orders to go ahead with it as the deadline for submissions is only two weeks distant.'

Miranda had been kneeling on the floor with her sketches of Francesca and the baby spread around her, and now she jumped up. 'Will I have to be involved?'

'Of course you will,' he said, surprised. 'The original concept is yours, after all, though the actual presentation of the design will, I think, have to be done by professionals. I'm on my way now to see the draughtsmen, and to put in hand a preliminary costing. Tomorrow the men will start making a small trial section. You'll have to be in on that, too.'

Her heart sank. That would mean more time in the fittings shop with bully-boy Lorenzo ready to make trouble.

'In the round-house, at first,' went on Ben, to her relief. 'Your design is more akin to the free-formed work done there than to the geometrical precision of the fittings shop.'

'Yes,' she said thankfully. 'I can see that.'

'Here's a cheque,' he said suddenly. 'An advance on the fee I promised you. It's for half a million lire, and if we work up something good enough to submit, I'll double it. If, by great good fortune, we gain the commission, there'll be a further fee and I'll see that you get full credit for the basic design. That, more than anything, will be of help to you in your career.'

'Thank you,' she said faintly. 'I never imagined I'd earn money from designing—at least, not yet.' Half a million lire sounded like a fortune, but was actually equivalent to just over two hundred pounds in English money. It was more than welcome, though, considering the state of her finances. 'I haven't a bank account here, Ben,' she said doubtfully. 'Can I cash this somewhere?'

'Of course.' He scrawled an alteration on the cheque. 'Take it to any bank in Venice.' He eyed her keenly. 'Are you all right for money, Miranda?'

'I am now, with this,' she assured him. 'I'll have enough for my fare home, when the time comes.' She looked up at him and ran a hand through her hair. 'You haven't yet said anything about whether you want me to stay on after my month's trial. Have you thought about it?'

To her dismay he gave her no assurance, but just said irritably, 'Of course I've thought about it. Frequently. But I can give you no definite answer. Not because of your work, which is excellent, nor yet because of your potential, which is immense, but because of this very delicate situation with the men.'

Miranda's eyes were startlingly blue in a face faintly gold from the previous day's sun. She stared at him without blinking. 'Is that why you specified a month's trial, because of the men?'

'Yes,' he said quietly, 'that's why. Though when I did so I had no idea you would arouse such antagonism.'

She took that as he meant it, without offence. 'Perhaps they'll like me a bit more if you win this commission. I mean because I'll have been designing, rather than actually working on the glass.'

'I hope so. There's keen rivalry between the top houses here, and there'll be prestige among their fellows for the men of the successful company As for your staying on, we'll both decide on that. A joint decision.

And I'll be responsible for your fare home, of course. It never occurred to me that you might imagine otherwise.' He looked at his watch. 'I'll see you later.'

'But what about our afternoon sessions? Are they to be discontinued, in view of all this extra work going on?'

'Certainly not. I'll see you at one in the polishing room. The racing yacht has to be ready for air-freight to the States by mid-week. As for the screen—someone from the drawing office will be in touch . . .'

He turned away for the second time, and noticed the sketches on the floor. He scooped them up and dumped them on her work-bench. 'What have you in mind here?'

'I thought I'd attempt a sculpture of a Madonna and Child,' she said simply.

'Based on Francesca and the baby? In what medium?'

'Just clay at first, and eventually—well—I don't know.'

He looked at her closely. 'I think you do.'

'A Madonna and Child in your father's new glass— the dei Santi gold.'

'Hah!' She knew that syllable. It indicated keen interest.

'There must be hundreds of Madonnas in Venice,' she said quickly, 'but so far I haven't seen one in glass. I know it's wildly ambitious and I can never manage it on my own. So I thought, when you aren't so busy . . .'

'Yes?'

'I thought, perhaps . . .' It was no use, she couldn't say it.

'You thought we could work on it together?'

'Yes,' she said.

'And so we shall, Miranda Brown. We'll make a glass Madonna. Together.'

With a hint of the dazzling smile touching his mouth

he ran back down the stairs, leaving her with one hand pressed to her chest, unwilling to admit that her heart seemed to have changed position again.

Innocenzo's work-room was a complete surprise. Knowing his ultra-modern macho image, Miranda had anticipated stainless steel, plastic, and electronic appliances by the dozen, not to mention a few nude pin-ups on the walls. Instead, the room was distinctly old-fashioned, with wood-working tools in immaculate ranks and shelves full of model-making equipment. As for the pin-ups—if they existed at all he'd taken them down before she arrived.

'Come in, Miranda. Perhaps you would sit here? May I offer you a coffee?' The usual flirtatious note was there, and she felt glad to be wearing her dungarees and a round-necked tee shirt. Innocenzo's beautiful eyes were apt to look her over very closely indeed.

'The Maestro has told me of your efforts to produce a design,' he said. 'And also that the old Maestro has now approved it.'

'That is so,' she agreed carefully.

'You have reconsidered, I see, about leaving the dei Santi enterprise?'

Of course . . . the last time they met had been in Ben's office, when she'd been all set to go home, and had said so. 'I rather think I'll stay, Innocenzo. That's if I'm asked. I'm still on trial, you see, until the end of next week.'

She missed his reaction to that, as he bent his head immediately. 'Is that so?' he said, politely surprised. 'You will know, Miranda, that nothing quite like this screen has ever been attempted here at dei Santi?'

'So I've been told.'

'It is—how can I put it—rather futuristic, is it not? But very beautiful. This sheet of drawings is the one from which I make models for the men?' As he spoke he was stroking a piece of pale, satin-smooth pine. Miranda watched the slim fingers caressing the wood, and wondered if he 'had no feel for the glass' because he was more at home with wood.

'Yes,' she said. 'The sizes are listed here. Each fish is detailed, and the Maestro wants a model of these four in particular ... Also, I wondered if you could make a ribbon of seaweed, similar to this one ...'

The next hour passed so pleasantly that she was amazed when the buzzer sounded for the lunch break. Innocenzo seemed a different person in the neat little room that smelled of wood and glue, and she thought she detected a baffled gleam in his eyes. Was he, like her, beginning to think that perhaps they could be friends? Real friends?

'I will proceed with all speed,' he assured her, holding open the door. 'You will come again tomorrow?'

'Yes,' she said readily. 'Thank you, Innocenzo.'

It was warm in the streets of Murano, and one of the rare days when the Alps were visible. The busy little street with its shops and neat houses ended at the lagoon's edge, and from across the water, looking far-distant and unreal, the snowy peaks gazed down on that bustling community of glass-workers.

'Look on it while you can,' Miranda told herself glumly. 'In ten days' time you might be back in Stourley.' She crossed the canal fronting Murano's lovely old Basilica, went on past the little grotto of remembrance at the foot of the bell tower, and headed for a place where she could eat her lunch in solitude.

She liked Murano on its five little islets; she liked its clean-swept streets and village-like atmosphere, and thought it a pity that most tourists went no further than the Rio dei Vetrai, with its cheap glass shops and its furnace-houses open to the public.

Cafés and houses and lines of washing left behind, she sat on a low stone wall and looked across the water, thinking that before long the screen would be taken out of her hands and dealt with by the dei Santi experts. She found she didn't mind; in fact she was relieved. She knew too little about the techniques of such work, and in fact felt a twinge of amazed pride that in such a short time her nebulous idea had become fact. She must keep an eye on the colours, though ... It must be subtle, subdued, without a hint of gaudiness ...

She opened her bag and looked again at Ben's cheque, still thrilled at the sight of her first fee. She could afford to buy presents for the family, and a new summer dress. Prices of clothes in Venice were beyond her, but there was material on sale, and if she could borrow Danielle's sewing machine ... And now she had extra money she could telephone home. It would be lovely to hear them all.

She bit into a crispy roll, and thought hard about the glass Madonna. Was there any point in starting on it, if she might not be here much longer? She stared out to where the Serenella canal merged with the bright lagoon. Instinct urged her to go ahead with it, if only as a sort of thank you to Ben for the efforts he'd made on her behalf.

Felicetta had been in the tower room that morning, asking after baby Paolo, and with a kind of studied casualness about Alessandro. They had spent ten minutes in friendly conversation, and in the course of it Felicetta had let slip that nowadays the Maestro was at his desk by seven a.m. and sometimes even earlier. That, Miranda knew, was because of her, so that he could spare the time for their afternoon teaching

sessions. Yes, she'd work on the Madonna, using some
easy to handle material, just to see if she could capture
the elusive quality shared by both Francesca and the
Bellini paintings.

Soon it was time to go back. Behind her was the
deserted church of the Angeli, now used only rarely, so
she'd read. She might as well have a look at it. She went
beneath an archway and found herself in a neglected
grassy area surrounding the old cream-coloured church.
It was very quiet. She could hear the splash of oars
from beyond the wall, and the faraway note of an
aircraft across the lagoon.

Then she heard voices, speaking quietly but urgently.
A young couple were in each other's arms, half-hidden
by overgrown shrubs. Reluctant to disturb them,
Miranda turned to leave. Then she stopped. The girl
looked very young, with shiny brown hair falling almost
to her waist. But the man! There was no mistaking that
improbable profile. It was Innocenzo.

Quietly she went back beneath the arch. The couple
shared an air of secrecy, almost of desperation, and had
chosen a meeting place where they were unlikely to be
seen. Perhaps the girl was considered too young for a
serious relationship, or Innocenzo unsuitable? Miranda
smiled. Hadn't she always felt that his overtures to
herself had been merely for show? Now she knew why.

She went back by a different route, hurrying now. It
would soon be one o'clock, and Ben dei Santi was
always punctual.

Miranda was in high spirits as she walked beneath the
walls of the Arsenal, heading for Celestia and another
week's work. Not, she told herself firmly, that her good
humour had anything to do with seeing Ben again after
the two-day break.

It had been a lovely weekend. She and Danielle had

spent ages shopping for material for a sun-dress, and
eventually decided on a fine cotton in a soft butter-
yellow. She'd treated them both to a ruinously
expensive coffee at Florian's in the Piazza, and then
they'd gone to see the famous bronze horses of San
Marco, prancing eternally in a quiet little room just
round the corner from their original place of honour
above the entrance to the Basilica.

She'd telephoned home, and had a talk with
everyone. Even Bobby had shouted down the phone
some incomprehensible baby-talk.

The Signora had offered her and Danielle the use of
her roof-garden, where they wrote up their notes at a
wicker table, and sketched out a style for a sun-dress.
An aged ex-gondolier had called on his friend the
Signora, and had kissed their hands, telling Danielle
that he had once been in love with a Frenchwoman, and
informing Miranda that her hair was like sunshine on a
field of golden grain.

They had laughed a little, afterwards, and Miranda
had tried, and failed, to imagine her great-uncle
Matthew doing and saying anything remotely similar.

With Spiro and Antoine she and Danielle had spent a
day on the Lido, the long island dividing the lagoon
from the sea. Miranda had been eager to go, not only
because it was Italy's most fashionable seaside resort,
but because she wanted to see the area where Elena
Comino lived.

Good-naturedly the others had trailed along with
her, though Spiro was evidently at a loss to understand
why someone who boarded a *vaporetto* to get away
from Venice, should then spend ages looking back at
the glistening pink city across the water.

At the Porto di Lido, the main entrance to the
lagoon, he'd sat on a wall and watched Miranda rather
than the view. Oblivious to the others, her hair flying

back banner-like in the wind, she'd watched an ocean liner pass through the Porto, heading for Venice. 'Just think, Spiro,' she had said, 'ships have passed through this channel for a thousand years. And it was here that the Venetians used to throw great chains across the water to prevent their enemies entering the lagoon.'

Spiro had been unimpressed by their sightseeing, but it had been such an interesting weekend she'd almost managed to push Ben to the back of her mind ... almost ... She'd climbed the stairs to her room and examined her early efforts with the Madonna. The first impression was there, roughly formed in clay, and she'd stared at it intently, seeing what it could become if she did everything right, slipped on an old shirt and the open sandals she used now that it was so much warmer, and had begun her next version of the Madonna.

Much later she tied back her hair in preparation for a visit to the furnaces, feeling less reluctant than usual because the men had been almost civil the last time she was there. Tucking a roll of drawings under her arm for delivery to the draughtsmen on her way back, she went down to the yard.

There were ladders up against the round-house, where men were at work on the intricate tiling of the roof, and she waved to Baldassare when she saw him carrying in lengths of guttering from the water-gate. Inside the building the familiar smell came to her like a welcome; faintly metallic, hot and dry and dusty. It was darker than usual opposite furnace number two, and she saw that boarding was covering the outside of the high window, where men were repairing the roof.

She went across to number four furnace and felt her sandal come loose as she walked. The buckle had come off—she'd have to go back in a minute to change into her shoes. Loose footgear wasn't safe so near the furnaces.

From where she stood the blocked-off window with its wooden backing acted almost like a mirror. She saw the reflection of Innocenzo approaching her from behind, but didn't turn to greet him as she was watching Tommaso and his team tackling a long ribbon of glass seaweed. She edged sideways, out of everyone's way, and tucked the roll of papers further under her arm.

A silence seemed to have descended on the high, round building. The men had stopped singing, and she could hear a radio playing nearby, sounding tinny and off-key beneath the dull roar of the furnaces. She watched Tommaso flatten the ribbon of still-flexible glass on the marver, and for some reason glanced up again at the window. Innocenzo's face was reflected there in profile, looking at someone behind her. She saw him nod his head deliberately.

Curious and suddenly uneasy, Miranda whirled round. She felt her loose sandal slip and she lurched sideways, off balance. There was a blinding sweep of light, and searing heat behind her neck. What——? Someone shouted, then a powerful blow knocked her to the floor. As she went down she glimpsed Innocenzo's face, shocked and horrified, his mouth a round O of dismay.

She could hardly breathe. Her head was covered in sacking. There was a smell of burnt hair, and the back of her neck hurt. Somebody was screaming, a high, thin sound. She swallowed dusty air and felt grit on her tongue. The screaming stopped. It had been her!

At the same moment she heard blasts on the works hooter. The accident call for the round-house! She moved her head under the sacking and felt the nerves of her neck scream into life. She'd been burned! She heard voices, babbling and confused. Why didn't somebody lift her up?

Then a familiar voice, groaning in unbelief. 'God above! You didn't touch her with the glass? What—just her hair?' Gentle hands removed the dusty sack. 'Miranda. This is Ben. Keep still for a moment. It's all right. I'll take care of everything.' Shakily she raised herself on her elbows, and heard him giving orders. 'Tommaso, get the stretcher! Armani—the burn dressings! Send Antelami to the launch. Bring a blanket—she's in shock!'

She felt the moist mesh of a sterile dressing against her neck, and a sob of pain and horror escaped her. She felt cold and very clammy. Then something warm and soft was slipped beneath her face. 'Don't try to move,' said Ben's voice, close to her ear, and thankfully she laid her face against the smooth material. Beneath the smell of dust and burnt hair she caught the odour of it. Fresh, male, faintly spicy. It was Ben's shirt.

Smiling weakly, she lay there. He was here. Why had she panicked? And then he was kneeling beside her, his warm hand on hers. 'Miranda. We'll have you out of here in just a moment. No, don't move. There's been an accident. Your hair caught fire—thank God you'd tied it back. The men knocked you down and smothered the flames.'

Someone lifted her and placed her, still face down, on a stretcher. She clutched the shirt and buried her face in it. 'Right,' Ben said. 'To the water-gate, quickly.' Her head was reeling and she felt sick. Then she was carried along the arcaded walkway, and she heard his voice behind her, saying with flat, deadly calm, 'I want to see every man in turn when I get back. Warn the hospital that we're coming, and send Felicetta after us with the signorina's papers.'

She was put aboard, and Baldassare touched her hand in wordless comfort. With a deafening roar the launch set off across the lagoon. She knew that Ben was by her side, because he still held her hand. She heard him say, 'Faster, Baldassare, faster,' and the boatman reply, astonishingly, 'She will go no faster, Maestro. *You* brought her to Murano, the little signorina. You knew there was risk.'

She felt Ben's fingers go rigid, but he made no reply. She wanted to see his face, but couldn't make the effort to turn her head. The launch swirled to a halt at the hospital landing stage, and uniformed figures carried her inside. Sheer good fortune, she thought hazily, that the hospital was facing Murano. There was the familiar smell, the orderly calm, the squeak of rubber soles on polished floors.

Efficient fingers lifted her hair. She wondered how much of it was left. 'Remove this,' said a cool voice, and she felt scissors snipping busily behind her ears. She thought she heard a man say 'Aaah,' as if in pain, but her head was whirling again and she couldn't think who else could be hurt.

Then another voice, 'Maestro—leave us, if you please.' And a door opened and shut. Someone removed her shirt and then gave her an injection. 'For the pain, signorina, a little prick ... and for a short time only, an intravenous drip ...' Then her neck was cleaned and dressed, and she managed not to scream. A moment later another injection, a slow one this time, in the muscle of her thigh. 'Antibiotics, signorina ... a mere precaution ...'

Later, the kind voices assured her that all was well, and though a little bit had been trimmed off her hair it would soon grow again. They turned her on her side and cleaned an injury to her cheek. So that was why her face had felt so sore ...

Then, still on her side and wearing a hospital gown, she was in bed in a quiet room with the shutters closed. A muttered conversation was going on by the door, and she caught odd words, 'Shock, but not severe . . . rest and quiet . . . No, no cause for alarm . . . For a moment only, Maestro.'

She opened her eyes to see Ben by the bed. He was wearing his shirt again. She could remember trying to hang on to it, but the nurse had taken it away . . . She wondered what they'd put on his face to give it that white, powdery look.

'Miranda,' he said carefully, 'you will fall asleep soon, because of the injection, so I have only a moment to speak. They tell me there will be no permanent damage to your skin, but do you know they have had to cut your hair?'

She looked at him and felt her heart move as surely as if someone had opened up her chest and pushed the still-beating organ to a different position. Instinctively, she knew that he felt he'd failed in his self-appointed responsibility for her well-being. She wanted to answer him, but her lips felt rubbery and hard to control. 'Don't worry,' she said slowly. 'My hair—I don't mind. I'd been thinking of having it cut.'

His response to that was to kiss her hand. It was always her hand, she thought crossly, never her lips. 'Miranda,' he said urgently, 'I have to telephone your father. Have you any message?'

The look on his face was awful. She couldn't let him tell Dad that she'd been burned in his glasshouse. 'No!' she said clearly. 'No. Don't ring Dad. It's not necessary. I'll be all right.' She raised herself on an arm. 'Don't ring him!'

'All right,' he said quickly. 'Don't move. Don't get upset. I won't ring your home—at least, not yet.'

She sighed in relief, and tried to remember what she must tell him. The awful face looked at her wordlessly. All bone and no flesh beneath that paper-white skin. She couldn't bear to see it so she closed her eyes. She had to tell him something—what had she wanted to say? 'I want——' she began, 'Innocenzo ... Innocenzo ...'

'He isn't here, Miranda,' said Ben quietly.

'I know that. But——' Her mind groped beneath waves of sleepiness, and she forced open her eyes and looked straight into his. They were dark and cloudy, not clear as they usually were ... Then she remembered what she wanted to say. 'Benvenuto ...' She liked saying that so she said it again. 'Benvenuto ... not deliberate ... it was an accident ...' She thought for a moment. 'My sandal came loose ... I stumbled ...' Then she made her final point. 'You—are—not—responsible.'

Pleased at remembering all that, she smiled, until she found that smiling made her face hurt even more. She saw that Ben seemed incapable of speech, but at last he spoke, and she knew she was imagining that his voice trembled. 'Felicetta is here with me, Miranda. You are to be kept in hospital for a day or two, under observation. Do you want anything brought in?'

She looked past him to where the small, composed figure waited. 'Nighties,' she said vaguely. 'Washing things ... toothbrush ... a comb?' Her hand wavered upwards towards her head. 'Danielle. Ask her to come, with her scissors.'

The door opened. 'Maestro,' said a voice, politely.

She didn't want him to go. 'Stay,' she whispered, putting out her hand. 'Please stay.'

'I'm here,' he said quietly.

Her eyelids closed. Someone put soft pillows down the bed to prevent her turning and lying on her back, and she drifted into a drugged sleep, in which the only comfort was the warm hand holding hers.

CHAPTER TEN

'No, Danielle—cut it short all over, like a boy's.' Miranda wanted no elaborate camouflage of her hair. It looked so awful that she was sure a close crop could only improve it.

The other girl still hesitated, clearly appalled at the task. 'Perhaps you should call in a qualified hairdresser?'

'I might do that later. Right now I can still smell burned hair. Just snip away, there's a love.'

Obediently, Danielle tried to bring order to the ruined, corn-coloured mess. 'Your ears are small and flat, anyway,' she said consolingly, 'and your head is well-shaped for such a style. Even so, I don't know how you can take it all so—so calmly.'

'I wasn't too calm when it happened,' said Miranda, remembering. 'But when I wakened up in the night I found I wasn't all that upset.'

'Were you alone?'

'Yes. They told me Ben dei Santi was here from eight until midnight, then they made him leave. I wakened about one and asked for something to eat, so they gave me a lovely supper, then I went back to sleep until this morning. Do you wonder I feel a bit better?'

'Well, you seem pretty fit now,' agreed Danielle doubtfully. 'I imagined the worst when I heard the news. We were all horrified. Spiro was in quite a state.'

'I know. For once he was almost speechless when he brought his flowers in this morning. It was a relief when they let him stay for only a minute.'

Danielle snipped busily, but lifted her eyes to look at

140

the massed bowls and vases of blooms; the elaborate, expensive arrangements. 'I've never seen so many flowers in one room,' she said. 'Who sent them all?'

'The men in the round-house, where it happened; the dei Santi family in Verona; all of you at the Signora's; Elena Comino who's in Rome; Baldassare and his wife; Innocenzo Paulucci; the pink roses in the shape of a heart from Spiro, and the tall blue and white ones are from Ben dei Santi.' She thought again of the card that had accompanied them. No message. Just the one word in the familiar writing: *Benvenuto.*

Danielle was intent on Spiro's offering, transparently romantic and expensive. 'I see you have this one right next to your bed?'

Miranda shrugged rather guiltily. 'I felt awful about him spending all that money when he's so hard up,' she explained. 'The least I could do was to appear bowled over by his flowers.'

'Mm. I suppose so.' Danielle turned to the larkspur-like spires mixed with tall white daisies. 'These from Ben dei Santi look very English, somehow. The blue ones are the exact colour of your eyes, did you realise that?'

'No,' said Miranda blankly. 'I can't say I did. They were there when I woke up.'

'Miranda.' Danielle was hesitant. 'Are you going to go back? To the glassworks, I mean. It *was* an accident, wasn't it?'

Miranda looked into the dark, intelligent eyes. 'Yes, it was. The men were horrified. But as for going back there—I'll have to talk to Ben about it.' She was reluctant to discuss it with Danielle. In fact, at that moment she was deeply reluctant to discuss it with anyone at all, and she sat in silence as the thick locks of her hair fell to the floor.

'That's it,' said Danielle at last, stepping back. 'The best I can do. Do you want to look at yourself?'

Miranda examined her reflection. There was a livid bruise on her cheek and a red graze on her chin; mauve shadows circled her eyes, and her hair lay in thick, uneven ridges very close to her head. She looked terrible, and what was more, freed from the weight of all that hair she felt shivery and light-headed.

'It will settle down soon, I think,' said Danielle uneasily, 'but perhaps a razor cut would have been better.'

'It's fine. Thanks a lot, Danielle. Off you go or you'll be late for your lecture.'

As the door closed behind her friend Miranda sank back in the chair. Her knees still felt a bit wobbly. She looked out to where the sun was touching the lagoon with gold and cudgelled her brains into reluctant action. She needed to think very hard about what had happened before Ben came again.

She knew she'd been well away from any man with glass on his rod, just as she knew that she hadn't imagined the ominous silence which fell just before it happened. Neither had she imagined the reflection that by sheer chance had shown in the window. Innocenzo had nodded to the men—given them some sort of signal—she'd seen it.

But whatever he had signalled, she had also seen the horror and astonishment on his face; heard the dismayed gabbling of the men. There could be only one logical explanation for it all. They had intended to do something to frighten her; perhaps set fire to the papers she carried . . .

They hadn't bargained on her seeing the reflection, on her being so uneasy that she whirled round and set her hair swinging, and they certainly hadn't expected her to stumble sideways . . . Even so, they must have known they risked hurting her; and for it to be at Innocenzo's instigation . . . She'd thought that the past week of working with him had laid the basis of a friendship. How wrong could she be?

But even if all this supposition was correct, what should she do about it? All her instincts urged her to confront the men and sort things out once and for all. But that would mean Ben getting to know what they'd been up to ...

The nurse came in, talkative and purposeful; and although she felt distinctly short of energy to take a bath and have her hair washed, Miranda got out a clean nightie and the soap and talc that Felicetta had given her, and followed the energetic, white-clad figure into the bathroom.

When Ben arrived at midday she was sitting by the window wearing a skimpy blue nightie under her short towelling robe and feeling relieved that her hair no longer smelled revolting. He was wearing one of his superb suits, as if he'd been out on business, and looked much as usual, making her wonder if she'd imagined his ghastly paper-white colouring of the day before. Only the eyes were different, she thought. The alert glitter had gone, leaving them dull, almost opaque.

It was disconcerting when he offered her no greeting, but just stood inside the doorway, looking at her. 'Hello,' she said at last. A faint flush came up under her pallor as she recalled that yesterday she'd clutched his hand until she fell asleep. Self-consciously she fingered her damp hair. 'Thanks for the lovely flowers.'

He ignored that completely. 'How do you feel now, Miranda?'

'Oh, much better. You didn't telephone my father, did you?'

'No. Not as you seemed so set against it, although I wouldn't have alarmed him unduly.'

'I know. I think they might discharge me to-day, or

at the latest, tomorrow morning. Ben—about this room—it's private, isn't it? I'm not sure how I stand with insurance, or even if I'm covered for this sort of thing.'

He waved a hand impulsively. 'I think I can manage a paltry bill from the hospital, considering you were injured in my employment.' Then he said, his tone in gentle contrast to his attitude, 'The doctor is pleased with you, but he's warned me that you need several days of complete quiet when you leave here.'

'I see.' But she didn't, not really. What was he getting at?

'What do you think of your hair?' His manner was definitely odd, she decided. What did he expect her to think of her hair? That it was gorgeous?

'It's not as bad as I expected,' she said, 'and it grows quite quickly.'

'I should have made clear to the staff here that they must send for a qualified hairdresser.'

'Danielle is very good,' she said defensively. 'I know it looks awful, but I can go to a proper salon in a few days' time.'

He shook his head. 'As a matter of fact it looks extremely attractive. Does your neck give you pain?'

'Just a bit,' she conceded. 'But I'm lucky it wasn't very much worse. I do realise that.'

'So do I,' he said heavily. He began to prowl the room. Absently he read all the labels on her flowers, then said slowly, 'About Innocenzo, Miranda——'

'Yes?'

'You were asking for him, last night.'

'Was I?' She couldn't remember that.

'He won't be able to visit you. He went home, apparently unwell, before I returned to the works. He doesn't yet know what's the matter with him.'

Guilt? suggested a cynical voice in Miranda's mind.

Remorse? Or perhaps he needed a breathing space in which to concoct a plausible story? 'It doesn't matter,' she said listlessly. 'I'll see him later.'

He made no reply to that, but continued to pace the room. 'I'm afraid that in all the upheaval yesterday I didn't fully express my deep regret at what happened.' His eyes held hers. 'I'm sorry, Miranda.'

For the second time in ten days she watched those lips frame an unaccustomed apology. Her heart shifted. Was this why he was so edgy? Was he still holding himself responsible? She must put him at ease, once and for all. 'It was my fault,' she said firmly. 'I was clumsy. Don't imagine that I think any responsibility rests with you. My neck will heal—without a scar, so they say—and my hair will grow again.'

She felt a deathly tiredness seep into her limbs. If only she could have twenty-four hours to herself to gather her wits, instead of all this stress and subterfuge. With an effort she summoned up her wide, beautiful smile. 'Please, Ben, I mean it. Don't apologise.'

He stood by the window, gazing out, much as he'd done that Sunday morning in his apartment on the Grand Canal. 'You've very generous, Miranda,' he said simply.

She crushed the urge to ask if he'd spoken to the men. Quite clearly she recalled his words as she was carried away on the stretcher, 'I want to see each man in turn when I get back . . .' She could guess the version he'd been given, however many men he'd questioned.

Then he said, 'In May each year the servants open up the summer villa on my island in the lagoon. I wondered if you'd like to go there to recuperate for a few days?'

'You have an island in the lagoon?' For a moment she felt almost lively. First a world-famous glasshouse, then a place on the Grand Canal, now an island!

'Just a small one, not far from San Francesco del Deserto. There's an old *palazzo* which once belonged to a nobleman of Venice. It had fallen into ruin so I bought it and had it restored. It's very quiet there in the summer when Venice is packed with tourists, and Baldassare's wife, who has nursing experience, is willing to go there to look after you.'

Miranda's imagination summoned up the little island with its palace dreaming the summer away in the far reaches of the lagoon.

'And I think Elena might agree to come back from Rome to keep you company for a few days,' he added.

Caution slowed her racing pulse. 'Do I have to decide now?'

'No, of course not. It's just that I'd like you to have a quiet interlude before facing the journey back home.'

She felt her face go cold as the colour left it. 'You've decided, then? About not keeping me on after the month's trial?'

'Yes. I have,' he said flatly.

'But——' The colour came back to her cheeks in a flush of anger and dismay. 'But you said that whatever the decision might be we'd make it together. That's what you said.'

'I know it. I'm sorry to have reached it alone, but I can't believe you want to stay.'

Until that moment she'd not known *what* she wanted. But now—— 'Yes,' she said recklessly. 'As a matter of fact, I *do* want to stay!'

The observant eyes watched her, remote and very tired. 'I'm sorry, Miranda. I can't risk it.'

She blinked back tears of humiliation. So the men had won, after all. He wouldn't risk keeping her on and upsetting them further. Vainly she searched her mind for a reply, then to her dismay she felt her lower lip tremble and the hot tears slide down her cheeks.

Without a word he rang for the nurse. She arrived almost at once, and he said without preamble, 'I regret that I have inadvertently upset your patient. Perhaps she will need to rest? I'll call in again this evening, Miranda.' He opened the door and she could see Spiro standing there, looking dishevelled and distinctly put out at being faced by Ben.

She watched them both, and realised quite clearly that dealing with the tempestuous young Greek was a rest-cure compared to dealing with the calm and self-contained Ben dei Santi.

He departed without a backward look. The nurse ushered a resentful Spiro back into the corridor, then returned and helped Miranda into bed. 'I will just take the temperature, Signorina,' she murmured persuasively.

The roof-garden was warm in the afternoon sun. Miranda, by now tanned a pale gold, was wearing her new sun-dress and working on her final drawing of the Madonna. Down below a work barge chugged along the canal and she could hear Signora Gaspari's cracked soprano raised in song as she bustled about after her afternoon nap.

Much had happened since Miranda's stay in hospital. A high temperature had kept her there for three extra days, during which all visitors had been regimented in and out for brief, strictly-timed visits. Not surprisingly, Innocenzo Paulucci had not been among them, but if Ben noticed his absence, he made no comment.

She had turned down Ben's invitation to stay at his island villa. 'I don't think so, Ben,' she told him calmly, as if the decision hadn't cost her hours of sleep. 'I'll be quite all right at the Signora's, where I can see my friends.'

The black lashes remained lowered. 'Just as you

wish,' he said evenly. 'Though I must insist that you avoid any occasions that may tire you, and submit to a little extra care.'

That was the tone of all their conversations, polite but weighted with a new restraint. He seemed anxious not to upset her, but immovable in his intention to send her packing at the earliest opportunity.

She could hardly bear the thought of leaving him for good, although she told herself repeatedly that it was the most sensible solution. Even his apparent concern for her welfare couldn't make the situation seem less futile. They were far apart in culture, background and position; and he'd never once acted in any way other than that of a considerate employer.

Belatedly keeping his promise about joint decisions, he now discussed everything with her. Everything, that is, except what really happened that day in the roundhouse, and what the men had told him about it. The episode, it seemed, was over, finished, as if it had never been.

He had given her the second payment for the screen design, and brought the final drawings for her to see before they were submitted, sitting at the foot of her bed while she stayed propped against the pillows, with the bruises on her face by then fading to yellow and grey.

She saw that the draughtsmen had done her proud, with a series of beautifully mounted drawings and a full-colour presentation of her original design. 'This is gorgeous!' she said, leaning forward to study it as it lay on the bed across her legs. 'They've caught the essence of it exactly. Who did it, Ben?'

'I did,' he said with a faint smile. 'Years ago I worked frequently on this sort of thing. The men have made their specimen section, so Innocenzo and Tommaso are taking the lot to Rome tomorrow.'

Yes, a great deal had happened in the last ten days
... With Ben's second cheque she now had more money
than at any time in her entire life, and as for the screen
itself, he had masterminded the whole project and yet
managed to keep it uniquely her idea. She was indebted
to him for that, she knew, but did it really matter? She
would be back home long before the Marine Insurers
made their final choice.

Signora Gaspari had watched over her like a hen with
one ailing chick, ushering visitors in and out with much
clucking and presenting of cups of coffee. Felicetta had
called each afternoon, and while they chatted in the sun
Miranda had learned more about the dei Santi family,
and gained a perverse pleasure in hearing about Ben
from someone who had known him since he was a
child.

The secretary told her that he and Elena had been
close companions since her fiancé's death in the triple
drowning four years ago. Felicetta's husky voice had
been oddly gentle as she explained that the two of them
had always been close, and Miranda wondered if she
was trying to warn, to prepare her. Actually, she found
the information unsurprising. It was no more, or less,
than she'd imagined.

As the days passed she'd formed her own conclusions
about another matter—the relationship between the
young Felicetta and Alessandro dei Santi. She told
herself bracingly that the secretary hadn't got the man
she loved and wanted, yet she'd led an interesting and
independent life ...

Baldassare and his wife had visited her too, full of
their daughter's forthcoming marriage. They even
presented her with an invitation to the wedding, but
she'd had to refuse, explaining that in mid-June she
would be at home, taking her finals.

And one bright afternoon, Alessandro himself had

called after visiting the glasshouse, bearing masses of
flowers and a bundle of photographs from Francesca.
He'd been surprisingly gentle; full of graceful com-
pliments about her new hairstyle and asking her
opinion on the finalising of the designs for the screen.
Like everyone else, he made no mention of the accident.
After he'd gone she leaned over the railings and
watched the launch head along the canal towards the
railway station, wondering if she would ever see that
gaunt, wheezing figure again.

She wriggled impatiently beneath the sun unbrella
and decided she felt perfectly fit. Her neck was almost
healed and she'd finished attending the hospital out-
patients department. All she had to do now was avoid
getting the new skin sunburnt. Her hair looked quite
decent, too. She'd visited a salon near the Piazza, where
they'd worked wonders on it, feathering the clumpy
ridges away until she looked like a large-eyed urchin
wearing a close-fitting gold cap.

She stared at her drawing of the Madonna, then
turned to her final clay model, tucked away in the
shade. She knew it was good; she'd captured the
serenity, the dream-like tranquillity of a new mother
looking down at her baby. Miranda sat staring at the
young face, framed by its smooth, looped hair.

All at once her tough, British determination surfaced
after a fortnight's submersion. Why should she let herself
be shunted back to England as if *she'd* done something
wrong? Oh, no doubt the men were sorry she'd been
burned, but she was sure they'd breathed a joint sigh of
relief that she was out of the glasshouse for good.

She would go and see Ben about it. No—she couldn't
do that—by now he was living in his summer villa, out
in the remote reaches of the lagoon. She went down and
telephoned him at the office. 'Ben? This is Miranda. I'd
like to talk to you as soon as it's convenient.'

The deep voice held the infuriatingly patient note of the last two weeks. 'I can be with you in an hour, Miranda.'

'Oh. Right. I'll see you then.'

She went up to the garden again and poured herself a glass of lemonade. Then she took down her drawing and folded the easel away. No doubt Ben expected another of their polite, low-key conversations. Well, this time he was in for a surprise.

'But we've already decided against it!' He stood with his back to the railings, looking dark and extremely bad-tempered against the pale, cloudless sky. The discussion was as she'd envisaged, neither polite nor low-key.

'*You* decided, if you remember, not me,' she said flatly. 'If I go home without once showing my face over there I shall feel I've been packed off in disgrace. We both know I've got to go back in ten days' time at the latest to prepare for my finals. Why can't I go in to work until then?'

He almost snapped at her. 'Because I prefer that you don't.'

'Have you already told the men that I've finished, then?'

'No, as a matter of fact, I haven't.'

'Then *please* can I go in? Just for a week. I won't set foot on the shop floor, and I'll go back to England next weekend.'

'No. I'm sorry.' He drummed his fingers on the railing at his side, and stared deliberately over her head.

She turned away, thinking hard. She wasn't going to grovel, but it was his firm, after all.

Beside her on a stone ledge was the clay model of the Madonna, holding her baby. It seemed to Miranda that the serene features were viewing their argument with quite unjustified calm. She sighed, suddenly exhausted. Perhaps she wasn't as fit as she'd imagined.

Then Ben spoke, right behind her. He was so close she could feel his breath on the still-tender skin of her neck. 'You've finished your model of the Madonna? I didn't know that.'

She nodded. 'That's why I asked for all my stuff to be brought here. I've been working on it every day.'

His eyes, clear again now, observed her and glittered with interest. 'Did you do any more sketches?'

She pointed to the stacked drawings on the wicker table. What a waste of time they'd been, she thought wearily, and sank down in a chair out of the sun, while Ben examined the drawings with an odd look on his face.

He walked back and confronted the Madonna, then returned to the table. 'I don't make a habit of breaking promises, you know,' he announced irritably.

'I never said you did,' she replied, baffled. 'What do you mean?'

'I remember telling you that we'd make the glass Madonna—together,' he said. 'It was the day after we'd been to Verona.'

'I know it was,' she agreed, 'but I didn't take it as a solemn promise, or anything.'

'I never imagined you might still be working on it,' he said. 'Why did you? Carry on with it, I mean?'

'Oh, I don't know.' She fiddled with the bootlace strap of her sundress. 'Well—actually—I suppose I wanted to finish it as a sort of thank you.'

'A thank you?'

'For you. For all you did for me before—before the accident. It sounds a bit pretentious when I say it out loud, but I thought that if I left the model and all the sketches, you might one day use them as the basis for a sculpture.'

He shook his head and turned away abruptly. Then all at once he whirled round to face her. 'Look

Miranda, would it satisfy you to go back to the glasshouse next week? Not alone, you understand, but with me. To make the Madonna together.'

'Yes,' she said promptly.

'You do see that I can't have you wandering alone through the works?'

'Yes. But——' She looked up at him eagerly, 'Can I arrive on my own on Monday? Without anyone expecting to see me? I can't explain why, but I want to call on Innocenzo, briefly, in his workroom. I promise not to go near the furnaces.'

He seemed to be expecting that. 'Very well,' he agreed tiredly. 'But after that, you stay in your room, and only venture on the shop floor in my company.'

'Agreed,' she said, beaming.

'I'll see you in the tower at nine on Monday. We'll use number six furnace as soon as it's free. Enrico has already made samples of the dei Santi gold, so there'll be no problems there.'

Miranda stood in the shade, a shaft of sunlight touching her close-cropped hair. 'Thanks, Ben,' she said quietly.

'Miranda!' There was a clatter of feet on the stairs, and Spiro burst through the doorway. He didn't see Ben, but went straight to Miranda and planted a smacking kiss on one bare shoulder. 'We're all going out tonight. There's a boat race on and then a firework display in the public gardens. Say you'll come?'

'Yes,' she said, still smiling with relief at the outcome of her talk with Ben. 'I'll come. Ben's here, Spiro——' She turned to the other man, but he was already going. With a grave nod he left the two of them together.

'What did *he* want?' asked Spiro aggressively.

CHAPTER ELEVEN

ON Monday morning Miranda found the launch moored between the two little bridges, with Baldassare waiting patiently to transport her and the Madonna to the glasshouse.

'It is the Maestro's order,' he explained gravely. 'He believes you are not yet strong enough for public transport.'

Together they sailed across the sparkling lagoon, while Baldassare questioned her about how she was to spend the coming week. Reassured that she would never leave Ben's side, he smiled and put a blunt finger beneath her chin before he helped her ashore. 'I do not doubt that the men will be surprised to see you——'

She walked past the outdoor market, along the street of shops, and then turned towards the glasshouse. *'Buon giorno,'* she called brightly to the first dei Santi workmen she saw.

Their astonished expressions confirmed that they hadn't expected to see her again. The hulking figure of Lorenzo was in front of her, and she saw his bit-boy run to catch up with him; 'Passing on the news of my return', she thought grimly.

She made for Innocenzo's workroom. *'Avanti,'* he called, when she knocked. He was sitting by the open window, a piece of wood between his knees and a slim chisel in his hands. He was so intent on his work he didn't look up right away.

'Good morning, Innocenzo,' she said quietly.

He laid down the chisel very slowly, and stood up, turning to face her. 'Miranda,' he said, quiet as a sigh.

'You are back.' He surveyed her close-cropped hair, the faint remnants of bruising on her cheek, the shadow-circled eyes, the fined-down waist, and a dull red flush crept up beneath the perfect contours of his face.

'Oh yes. I'm back,' she said brightly. 'Didn't you expect me?'

'We—that is—I—er, no—I imagined you must soon return to England for your examinations.'

'That is so,' she agreed evenly, 'but first I have more work to do for the Maestro. Innocenzo—I've come to ask you what was going on that day when my hair was set on fire.'

He gaped at her. *'What?'*

'I saw you,' she said. 'I saw your reflection in the window as you nodded to the men. It was some sort of signal, wasn't it? What exactly were you telling them, Innocenzo?'

'I don't know what you mean,' he said abruptly. 'The Maestro—he believes you slipped sideways. That it was an accident.'

'Yes. I told him that. He knows my sandal was broken. What he doesn't know is that I saw you signal to the men just before it happened.'

'It is evident to me that your nerves are still on edge, Miranda.'

'Oh no. My nerves are quite all right,' she said, stretching the truth somewhat. 'You and the men planned to frighten me, didn't you? It was another attempt to get rid of me.'

The extravagantly long lashes came down, and she saw his lips tighten. When he looked up again she drew back from the open hostility in his gaze.

'Yes,' he said bitingly. 'It was another attempt to get rid of you. We don't want you here, Miranda Brown. We don't want foreigners—women—in our glasshouse, no matter how blonde and pretty they may be. We have always intended to get rid of you, from the moment you arrived here.'

Well, that was plain enough . . . the truth at last! 'But what have I ever done to you that you should risk burning me?'

'Pah! We saw no risk. The men have been handling molten glass all their working lives. They light their cigarettes with it, so well do they control their rods. We didn't expect you to turn so quickly, and set your hair swinging, and we didn't know you would overbalance. That is all.' For a second regret was there. 'We intended you no harm.'

'How reassuring,' she said quietly. 'It was sheer misfortune, of course, that I was burned, lost all my hair, and just missed being disfigured for life.' She went to the door. 'One day, Innocenzo, you and your workmates will *have* to accept women—and foreign women at that. The Maestro has known it for years, and I think the men know it must happen sooner or later. I suspect that you know it too, in your heart.'

Uncertainty registered on his face, and was quickly masked. She felt contempt rising. 'Why don't you admit that you're not right for the glass industry?' she asked scornfully. 'Why aren't you man enough to be independent—to start a woodworking business of your own? Then you could marry your girl-friend—the one you meet secretly in the churchyard of the Angeli.'

His jaw dropped, then he glared at her as the shot went home about being independent. 'Because I do not have the capital,' he said bitterly. 'I do not have the money, either to set up on my own or to marry into a wealthy family. I am related to the dei Santis—why should I not keep my position in the firm?'

'Because you're not right for it, Innocenzo, that's why. Surely you could ask the Maestro for a loan?'

'But——' he was spluttering with fury,' But this is no concern of yours!

'No,' she agreed wearily, 'it isn't.' She turned and left the workroom with its smell of wood and glue and wax, closing the door behind her with a dull, final click. He was right. It was no business of hers what he did with his life, and why she should have the urge to advise him about it she had no idea. With luck she wouldn't see him again before she went back to England.

Once in the tower room she threw wide the shutters, and as always, the four glorious views were there; ageless and enchanting. And with only five more days in which to look at them.

The air was hot and dry, the furnace was roaring and Ben was at her side, shirtless and wearing faded denims.

'Ah-hay!' At that command two of Armani's men helped him carry the white-hot glass from the pot to the marver, and were then waved back to their own team.

Bathed in sweat, Miranda stood at Ben's side as he sat at the iron slab. It was her last day, and this was their third and final attempt at making the Madonna.

For what seemed the hundredth time she sprayed her clay model with tepid water to prevent it cracking in the searing heat, and saw the tranquil terracotta features glow for an instant beneath the film of moisture.

'Take the rod!' instructed Ben. 'That's right, over here. Now this one as well. We need to centre it so, do we not?'

Throughout the week he had treated her as an equal when they were in the round-house, but outside it the constraint between them was still there; unmentioned, unacknowledged, but weighting their every exchange with tension and unease.

At the furnaces, though, it was different. As they'd approached number six for their first attempt he'd said,

'I can do this alone, you know, but the finished Madonna will have no life, no soul, no inner feeling. I can't convey it—that's why I've always done abstract or impressionist pieces. You will have to help me. Together—together we may manage it.' The crystal-like eyes had held hers, clear and compelling as always, but with a hint of appeal in their depths.

After that she found she was able to suggest, to improvise, to *explain*. It seemed incredible that a student should be able to explain anything at all to a man of Ben dei Santi's experience, but he seemed to find nothing demeaning in taking her advice and acting on her suggestions. His technical skill was immense, almost unbelievable; it was only in interpreting the emotions behind the features that he needed her help.

By mutual consent their first two attempts had been discarded after joint analysis of their flaws. Now, lack of time gave urgency to their efforts.

'Benvenuto,' she said, close to his ear. 'Her lips—can you make the lower one more full—to show how she loves her baby?'

He glanced across at the clay model, then up at Miranda. Her forehead was damp, the short hair flattened to her skull, and her concentration was such that she held her mouth in the curve she wanted to see on the Madonna—faintly smiling, the lower lip thrust out protectively as she looked down at the baby.

Ben watched her face for a mere instant, then leaned forward and with his smallest rod curved the molten lips into an exact replica of Miranda's.

'That's it!' she said tensely. 'And her neck, bent slightly more, do you think? Lovely! Oh—lovely!' She gripped the flexible gaspipe, ready to play the flame over the glass should it become too rigid, while Ben filled out the infant's cheeks and rounded his chin, glancing from his work to the clay version and back again.

Miranda breathed in the dry, metallic smell, braced herself against the blast of the furnace, and felt the tremendous heat of the molten Madonna. If she lived to be a hundred and never touched glass again, nothing, *nothing* could take away from her the excitement and sheer creative force of this time at the furnace with Ben. The strength of his hands on the rods, the immediacy of the work—the vital 'now' of glass; and finally the extreme delicacy with which he had just formed the Madonna's mouth.

Her sleeveless top was sticking to her back and her thin skirt clinging to her thighs. The big, lean hands next to her moved with such speed and precision she felt almost dizzy.

And then it was over. She heard Ben's breathing become slower, and her own chest rose and fell at a similar rate. Between them the Madonna relinquished her last hint of red, and faded to the subtly-tinged dei Santi gold.

Ben got up and ran his fingers through his damp hair. 'Will she do?' he asked intently.

Miranda looked at the Madonna and child. The features closely resembled those of Ben's sister Francesca and her baby Paolo, with a hint there of the Bellini Madonna. Yet, unmistakably, around the mouth, was a fleeting likeness to *her*—Miranda Brown!

She could see, though, that whoever the Madonna might resemble, she was, unmistakably, *right*. Excitedly she turned to Ben. Dark blue eyes met glittering grey ones, while behind them the furnace roared unceasingly. 'She'll do!' they said in unison.

His warm hand felt for hers, and he lifted it and touched her palm with his lips. As always, her fingers curled protectively over the spot he'd kissed. Then, because the emotion of the moment still held her, because she knew she might not see him for much longer, and perhaps because kisses on her hand fell short of what she really wanted from him, Miranda stood on tip-toe and planted a soft kiss on his jaw. It was meant for his cheek, actually, but she aimed too low. 'Thank you, Benvenuto,' she whispered.

His expression prevented her from saying more. He was annoyed. More—he was angry. She saw his teeth clamp tightly together as his gaze flicked beyond her to where the men were working beyond the partition. Honestly, she thought desolately, it was only a mere peck on the chin—a 'thank you'.

Almost at once he was his usual self again; a faint, derisive smile touching his lips as he picked up his shirt from where he'd tossed it minutes before. She watched him fasten the buttons over the hairs and muscles of his chest, and told herself quite calmly that she was seeing it for the last time.

'Come,' he said, freeing the wheels beneath the slab that held the Madonna. 'Let's take her to Carlo at the lehr.'

With a sense of finality that was too empty for despair, Miranda placed her hands next to his on the steel handle, and helped push the Madonna and Child to the cooling ovens.

It was a clear, sunny afternoon, so that Miranda could look down from the plane and see all too distinctly what she was leaving behind.

Far below was the close-packed pink city, divided by the double curve of the Grand Canal, and there—she sagged back in her seat, suddenly bereft—there was the tiny island of San Giorgio Maggiore with its red and white monastery and its spread of dark green trees. Ben had asked her to 'save it' for him, so that he could show her the view from the campanile. And she had done just that . . . deliberately kept away from the place, and for what? He'd never so much as mentioned it again.

Their farewells had been awkward. Polite, of course, with each of them thanking the other, but strained because she knew he couldn't wait to get her out of Venice, and she resented it bitterly.

'Baldassare will take you to the airport tomorrow,' he had told her, handing over her air-ticket. 'The small pieces you've made on your own should by now have arrived at the college, and I've sent Bill Wardle the official authentication that they're all your own work. Also, I've informed the EEC that your spell in Venice is at an end. I wish you success in your finals, Miranda. You deserve it.'

Her huge eyes had sought his. Was this to be their last farewell, then? Here in the yard, with workmen passing and crates being stacked on to a trolley? She reminded herself forcibly that their parting would be of less significance to him than it would be to her. His words proved that—'Your spell in Venice is at an end . . .'

'I'll say goodbye, then,' she had said gravely. 'Thank you for everything.' She'd held out her small, capable hand, expecting the usual light touch of his lips.

But as if her fingers had conveyed her reluctance to accept any such gesture, he took hold of it and shook it firmly in the English manner. 'Goodbye for the present, Miranda. I had hoped to take you to the airport myself, but I have to head for Rome as soon as I can get away from here this evening.'

Rome. Well, that was no surprise, she had thought bleakly. Elena was there. 'That's all right,' she'd said lightly. 'My friends from the Signora's are hoping to see me off.'

'Is that so? Then Baldassare can pick you all up, and take you across together.'

Silence had fallen between them, while Ben watched her with that intent crystal-like gaze. 'You said "goodbye for the present",' she'd said hesitantly. 'Does that mean we'll meet again?'

'I'll be in touch,' he said crisply. 'Did you doubt it? To let you know the outcome of the screen competition, and how the Madonna responds to her polishing after her time in the lehr. Now—do you wish to bid goodbye to anyone in the works? Armani? Tommaso? Enrico?'

She had shaken her head. They had all been determined to get rid of her, and she wanted no farewells from them.

'You will see Innocenzo, though?'

'No. He and I have said all we want to say to each other. There's only Felicetta. *She* might be sorry to see me go.'

With that she had left him, but couldn't resist turning just once when she reached the offices. He was still there, standing full in the sun with his furnace-house behind him.

She'd made for Felicetta's office, and after a quiet farewell walked out through the gates of the dei Santi glasshouse, her final departure unnoticed and unremarked.

That night there had been a farewell party in a local *trattoria* followed by a noisy international get-together in the Campo San Zanipolo. Later, on the landing outside her room, an unpleasant scene with Spiro was only resolved by Danielle's staunch presence and the prospect of the Signora's imminent arrival. The young Greek went off, muttering in his own language, and leaving Miranda wondering why the wrong man should be so anxious to make passionate love to her and the right one content merely to kiss her hand.

Sleepless, she'd looked back on her time in Venice, recalling in detail all that had passed between her and Ben. She didn't toss and turn, didn't thump her pillow, seeking rest; she had just lain there, one hand beneath her cheek, looking up at the stars above the Campo

Due Ponti, remembering.

Seven of them had come to see her off at Marco Polo. All those who'd been there when she arrived at the Gaspari house except for the musicians, who were back in Verona, playing for the open-air opera.

The others were all talking at once as they had crossed the lagoon, so that nobody except Baldassare seemed to notice she was very quiet. The others climbed the steps to the quay fronting the airport, leaving Miranda and the boatman on their own.

'I'll be thinking of you at your daughter's wedding, Baldassare,' she'd said quietly.

'And we'll be thinking of you, little one, working for your examinations,' he'd replied, his beefy hands enclosing hers. 'Good fortune go with you.'

She felt horribly close to tears, and Baldassare knew it. She had given him a tight hug and kissed his weather-beaten cheek, then followed the others, leaving him moist-eyed behind the wheel.

She checked in and soon it was time to go to the departure lounge. The little airport had been all bustle and activity, with porters rushing back and forth to the landing-stages. She heard the roar of a boat's engine, cut abruptly as it approached the quay, and then her friends had crowded round with invitations to visit them if ever she was in their various home countries. They all kissed her and she kissed them back. Then Spiro had spun her round. 'And me, Miranda. Say goodbye to me.'

She'd smiled into his eyes, and felt a stab of relief that she would soon be free of him. He was so persistent, and yet so likeable that she'd been finding it more and more difficult to keep him at a distance. 'It's been an experience, knowing you, Spiro,' she said diplomatically.

He had gathered her to him and kissed her hungrily, his mouth hot and greedy on hers. So what, she thought. He was a bit much, but he was nice and uncomplicated. She put her arms behind his neck and kissed him back, and the two Dutchmen clapped their hands approvingly.

Then she had pushed herself free. 'I must go,' she said breathlessly. 'Thanks for coming, all of you.' She had bent to pick up her hand baggage and as she straightened up saw a man's figure go through the doors and out to the quay. But it was—— No, of course it wasn't Ben. He was in Rome. She hoped she wasn't in for a spell of imagining every dark-haired man she saw to be him.

With their noisy goodbyes in her ears and the feel of Spiro's kisses on her lips, she had walked through the barrier and waited for her flight to be called.

Once at Heathrow there was the sheer bliss of hearing her own language spoken on all sides, and as the train sped through the countryside she wondered how she could ever have imagined that anywhere else could equal England.

It was good to see her father's familiar figure waiting in the vastness of Birmingham New Street. 'Dad—oh, Dad! It've lovely to see you. Where are Betty and Bobby? At home?'

'Yes. He's a bit edgy today, cutting more teeth, Betty says, so he's playing in the garden. Tea will be ready when we get back.' He put her away from him. 'Your hair, pet! You've had it cut off! No wonder I hardly recognised you.' He laughed. 'Not that it doesn't suit you, and it's easier, I expect?'

With a father's acceptance of his daughter's whims he dismissed the matter, and she sighed in relief. She didn't want to have to explain about that to anyone.

He put her cases in the car and they left the city and headed for Stourley. When they stopped at a road junction he gave her another quick kiss. 'It's good to have you home, pet.'

Miranda fell back into routine almost as if she'd never been away. Almost—but not quite. When the local bus turned into Walsall Road she saw, in the clear lens of memory, a gondola swinging round to enter a broad canal, with the gondolier giving voice to his unique warning call. When letters dropped on the mat she saw old ladies in tall houses hauling up baskets that had been lowered to street level to collect their mail, and when Bobby rampaged through the back garden she remembered two little girls skipping across the terraced lawns of a villa high above Verona . . .

Her father was full of questions about the dei Santi glasshouse, but mercifully, both he and the family accepted without question that her time in Venice had been shorter than she'd expected. 'Just as well, love,' said Betty comfortingly. 'All that foreign food can't have suited you—look how you've lost weight. Here— have another piece of strawberry shortcake.'

At the college, she found to her relief that her fellow-students were too engrossed in the run-up to their finals to pay much attention to her. The girls admired her tan and were surprised about her hair; they remembered to ask about Venice in their coffee breaks, then rushed back to last-minute revision and the hectic preparation for their shows.

Even Bill Wardle, usually so acute and perceptive, had little to say except, 'Welcome back, Miranda. I've heard from dei Santi and he says your work over there was first class. You've done the college proud, it seems. Can we have a long chat about it when next week's over?' Then, baggy-eyed and with a hunted expression, he rushed off in answer to a summons from the furnace-room.

She sat her exams and found them easier than she'd expected, and then joined in transforming the utilitarian, dust-filled department into a place of visual beauty in which to display the finalists' work to the external examiners.

They spared no efforts. Clutter was banished behind drapes and backdrops; sketch-books were laid out and drawings mounted; the corridors were transformed by tented ceilings and fabric-covered walls, and each student was allocated their own separate display area for the end products of their years of work. Bill Wardle was never in his office for more than two minutes at a time, but eventually came a breathing space.

It was the last afternoon before the shows were to be examined, and Miranda stood in her own little area, adjusting her creations. Absently she slipped a length of rope through the belt loops of her denim skirt. It was getting really loose round the waist and she was tired of it balancing on her hip bones.

Critically she paced back and forth. She'd rejected any of her stuff that wasn't glass sculpture, and had finally chosen a moulded shape made before she left for Venice, some of the free-formed pieces she'd made at dei Santi's—fish, birds, abstracts—and of course the baby's head. To her, it still looked amateurish, but she had to admit to its having that strange subtlety of expression . . .

Each piece was on its own stand, carefully spot-lit and backed by lengths of ivory crepe that she'd bought in Birmingham. She stood back and felt a surge of dismay. There didn't seem to be much to show . . .

Moodily she trailed round the other work and saw glass that was coloured, striped, plain, sandblasted, sheeted, enamelled—a mass of work that was both exuberant and innovative. She came back feeling a little more cheerful. Hers seemed to be as good as any . . .

A passing second-year student called from the door. 'Miranda! Bill wants you in his office——'

She re-tied the rope at her waist and went beneath the draped awnings. The office door was open, and she could see Bill Wardle sitting on the edge of his desk, listening intently to someone in there with him.

Miranda stopped. There was no mistaking that voice. The American accent was as familiar to her as her own English one. It was Ben! Here—in the Black Country!

CHAPTER TWELVE

THE eyes of both men turned to the dishevelled figure in the doorway. Bill Wardle himself sounded slightly bemused when he said, 'Mr dei Santi has come to see you, Miranda.'

She didn't even hear him. Huge eyes shining, forgetting all about the tensions of her last few days in Venice, she said delightedly, 'Ben! What a surprise!'

'Miranda.' Just the one word, quiet and faintly sad. 'Are you quite well?' He sounded as if her continued good health was in some doubt.

'Yes, I'm fine. How lovely to see you.' Heavens, she'd better calm down. No wonder he looked a bit dumbfounded.

'I'm in England on business,' he said gravely, 'so I thought I'd come to the Midlands in time to see your final show, and also to bring you some good news.'

Bill Wardle looked curiously at each of them in turn, but Ben seemed to have forgotten he was there. 'Your design for the screen has been accepted by the Marine Insurance Company of the Serenissima, Miranda. Congratulations.' He put out his hand and shook hers ceremoniously.

Miranda felt so stunned she couldn't speak, but Bill Wardle made up for her. 'What's this, then?' he asked keenly. 'I didn't know you'd been designing over there.' He turned to Ben and laughed, highly pleased. 'She's in a daze,' he said, shaking his head. 'Perhaps you'd better tell me about it.'

Miranda stood there, listening to the man she loved give an account of how a student's work came to be submitted to one of the most prestigious companies in Italy.

Everything began to seem unreal. The brilliant sunshine outside the window, the sudden quiet in the department after days of frenzied activity, and Ben himself, standing next to her in dark linen trousers and a white cotton shirt. She'd been schooling herself to accept that she might never see him again, and here he was, dropping in at the college as casually as if he lived in the next town, rather than in Venice.

Then, to her acute embarrassment, Bill Wardle said bluntly, 'Well, Miranda has always been one of our star pupils, Mr dei Santi, but if she's as good as you make out I'm surprised you decided to let her go.'

Ben looked from one to the other in some surprise. 'Miranda hasn't explained the situation at my glasshouse? I see. Perhaps later I may enlighten you. For the moment, would you be good enough to excuse us, Mr Wardle? I want to talk to Miranda, and then, if you have no objection, perhaps I might see the students' work?'

Leaving the Department Head gratified but somewhat perplexed, he led Miranda briskly outside, rather as if he was the one who knew the way and she the visitor. Together they walked past the crowded car park to the rising ground beyond.

'You haven't told Bill Wardle about your hair being burned, then?' He sounded baffled. 'Why is that?'

'It didn't arise,' she said simply. 'Everyone just took it for granted that I'd decided to have it cut.'

'Including your family?'

'Yes.'

'But haven't they asked why you aren't returning to Venice?'

She smiled slightly, 'They've just accepted that the month's trial was sufficient for me, so I haven't enlightened them further.'

He was silent for a moment, then he said curiously, 'You showed little reaction to the news about the screen. Are you not pleased?'

'Of course I am, but a bit amazed as well. It's good of you to take the trouble to come and tell me in person. Thank you.' The words sounded wooden, artificial, as if this meeting was going to be like those before she left Venice—creaking with strain.

'It was no trouble. I've come from London by car, on my way to Birmingham, so I called here first, that's all.' He handed her one of his crested envelopes. 'Here's the fee I promised you, should we win the commission.'

She turned the envelope over and over, but didn't open it. Money was gravitating towards her at top speed, these days. 'Are the men pleased about the screen?' she asked quietly.

'Oh yes. They're pleased. Even Armani showed signs of excitement. The Marine Insurers had started examining the designs the day before you came home, you know; that's why I had to dash off to Rome, to answer some of their queries.'

'I thought you were going to Rome to join Elena,' she said weakly.

'I saw her there, yes, with her new fiancé. He seems a decent enough type—makes films—documentaries, I think. They're to be married in the autumn.'

She gaped at him. 'She's getting married? And not to you?'

He shook his head. 'No. Not to me. I thought I'd told you long ago that she's just a friend of the family.'

'Yes,' she agreed, 'so you did.' She looked at him carefully but all she could discern was a trace of the weariness that had shown itself before she left Venice.

'Have you heard from Paulucci?' he asked suddenly.

'Innocenzo? Me? No. Why should I?'

'The two of you seemed quite close, I thought.'

'Close?' She laughed, suddenly carefree. 'Oh no! All that flirting on his part was just for show. I always suspected as much. When I went in to work that Monday we—er—cleared the air. I told him to leave glass and set up on his own in a woodworking business.'

'Did you indeed? Well, he's certainly leaving glass as far as my company is concerned, because I've fired him. An event long overdue.'

So Innocenzo was out of the company which he thought owed him a living ... 'Did he ask you for a loan, Ben?'

'He did not. Which is just as well as I wouldn't have given him one. Why do you ask?'

'He's in love with a girl from a wealthy family, and he told me he has no capital, either to marry her or to start up his own business.'

'So?'

'So I thought you might lend him some. I don't much like him, Ben, but he's unhappy, he has no money, and he does have an outsize chip on his shoulder. I thought setting up on his own might be the answer for him, that's all.'

They lingered in the shade of a huge chestnut tree, looking out across the industrial sprawl of the Black Country. 'That's the road to Stourley, where I live,' she told him, indicating the heavy traffic passing the college. 'Ben—would you have time to visit my father and Betty while you're here? Perhaps for a meal?'

He turned on her the rare, spectacular smile. 'I'd like that very much, Miranda, but I return to Venice first thing in the morning. It would have to be this evening, and then only briefly.'

'That'll be fine,' she said, beaming. 'About the Madonna—is she out of the lehr yet?'

'Yes. I saw her yesterday. She's very beautiful, even

before her polishing.' He looked at his watch. 'We'll have to go back now, if I'm to see your work and be in Birmingham by four-thirty.'

And so Miranda had the intense pleasure of touring the department with Benvenuto dei Santi, while Bill Wardle demonstrated their latest equipment and her friends clustered behind them, hanging on Ben's every word.

He examined her own display minutely, then kissed her hand in full view of the entire department, saying, 'You're heading for a First, Miranda. Just see if I'm not proved right!'

As she waved him off she thought of how she'd told herself that outside his Venetian setting he would no doubt lose his appeal and seem quite ordinary. In fact, the reverse was true. Here in the Black Country he seemed more attractive, more compelling, than ever. She loved him.

With a little laugh of sheer excitement she went back inside to have a last look at her show, then threw her belongings together and set off for home. The bus had almost reached Stourley before she recalled how he'd bundled her ruthlessly out of Venice in order to pacify his men.

Betty rushed to meet her as she walked up the front path. 'Oh, I'm glad you're back, love. There's a friend of yours here and I think he wants to stay. He's brought a bed-roll with him, but I can't understand a word he says.'

Miranda looked at the yellow back-pack in the hall. Oh no—not today! 'It's all right, Betty. I think I know who it is. Where is he?'

'In the garden, playing with Bobby.'

Sure enough, it was Spiro, looking out of place and faintly exotic in front of her father's greenhouse. He jumped to his feet and grinned at her triumphantly. 'I am here! On Monday I begin a three-week course at the Institute of the City and the Guilds in London, so I come here to see you.' He looked at Betty and bowed. 'Your pretty Mama has offered me a place to lay my sleeping bag. Are you not pleased to see me, Miranda?'

Notions of Greek ideas on hospitality chased each other through her mind. She could hardly send him on his way when he'd only just arrived. 'Welcome to Stourley, Spiro,' she said summoning a smile. 'Excuse me while I have a shower and change my clothes. I won't be long.'

She was in her bra and briefs turning on a tepid shower when Betty came into the bathroom. 'I'm sorry, Betty,' she said contritely. 'I had no idea he was going to turn up. I left him in Venice and thought I'd never see him again.'

'He's keen on you,' said her stepmother. 'Anybody can see that. And is he good-looking! What nationality is he? Italian?'

'No, Greek. He was a guest at the boarding house in Venice, doing a course in stone restoration. I suppose we can hardly refuse to put him up for at least one night?'

'Of course he must stay,' said Betty, 'until Sunday if you like. Bobby's certainly taken to him . . .'

'There's something else. Ben dei Santi is over here— my boss from Venice. He's calling to see you and Dad some time this evening. He says he won't be able to have a meal with us, as he's a bit pushed for time.'

At that even Betty's placidity was shaken. 'Oh, my goodness! Things are a bit chaotic, you know, what with Bobby teething and the hot weather and Dick in a state about his 'A' levels . . .' She thought for a moment, then gave her good-natured smile. 'Oh—why worry? Let 'em all come!'

They were still at the table when Miranda heard Ben's car. She'd warned Spiro he was coming, in the hope that he would behave himself better than he usually did when Ben was around.

She snatched a look in the hall mirror. For once she was looking decent, thank goodness . . . tanned, subtly made up, and with her newly washed hair lying in soft waves all over her head. Her heart thudded as she opened the front door. 'Come in, Ben. We're still having our meal, I'm afraid.'

With some surprise she saw that he was tense. Surely he couldn't be nervous? She led him into the dining room, unable to conceal her pleasure that he was here at last, meeting her family.

Side by side with him in the doorway, she took in the scene as it must appear to Ben. Her father and Betty, both on their feet with hands outstretched to greet him; Seb and Dick looking up from their food as if they hoped they wouldn't be prevented from eating; Bobby in his high-chair clutching his plastic mug, and Spiro, perfectly at ease, spooning trifle into the child's open mouth.

She saw Ben's amazed stare, and how for a second he closed his eyes. 'Spiro's only just arrived, Ben,' she murmured. 'He's on a City and Guilds course.' Then introductions all round before he was persuaded to sit at the table and accept a cup of tea.

He bent his head politely to Spiro, admired Bobby, charmed Betty, revealed an adequate knowledge of electronics when chatting to Seb and Dick, assured Frank Brown that he had a talented daughter, and never once looked at Miranda.

She sat next to him and wondered why he'd agreed to come, when she had sensed his eagerness to leave before he even sat down. When he rose to his feet after ten minutes she felt vaguely surprised that he'd hung on for

so long. Had she dreamt that he'd seemed delighted at
the idea of visiting her family?

At the door she looked up at him. 'I'm sorry you
couldn't stay longer,' she said awkwardly.

'Why did you ask me here?' he demanded, his voice
low. 'Wasn't it enough that you have the Greek?'

'Spiro? But I told you——' she gasped.

'No doubt he is here to continue what you began in
Venice,' he said tightly.

'Began in Venice? What do you mean?'

'The sessions in your bedroom. The kisses on your
bare shoulders, the display of passion at the airport.'

'At the airport? Oh.' So it *had* been him, the man she
saw turning away after that clinch with Spiro. 'You
were there?' she asked, lifting uncomfortable eyes to his.

'Yes. I'd rushed back from Rome in order to bid you
a last farewell, but when I saw you with the Greek I
turned round and went back home. You needed no
more goodbyes after that one.'

She thought of the goodbye he'd given her the day
before she left Venice—an English handshake in the
yard with workmen all around them. 'We'd already said
our goodbyes to each other,' she reminded him. 'A
handshake, as I recall.'

'I remember,' he said tiredly. 'Perhaps if I'd tried a
different approach I might have received a response like
that you gave the Greek.'

Fury rose in her so suddenly it tightened her throat.
'The Greek?' she choked, 'he has a name, you know.
And what has it to do with you if I should decide to
kiss every man I meet?'

'What indeed?' he said, shrugging. The transparent
eyes looked cold and dull as stones. 'I have to see
someone in London this evening, and I'm already late.
Goodbye, Miranda.'

'Goodbye!' She slammed the door behind him, then

stood in the hall, gathering her wits before returning to the table to pretend that all was well.

Later, doing the washing-up, she said, 'I'm sorry Ben's visit was a bit awkward, Betty. I think he must have been a bit put out to find Spiro here.'

Betty looked up from the sink, her face bright pink from the heat and the washing-up water. 'Is he married?' she asked. First things first, with Betty.

'No. Why?'

'Because he was jealous,' said the older woman calmly.

The idea came to her during the night, urgent and unmistakable, born during the long hours of question and answer going on in her head while the rest of the household slept. Had Ben really imagined that she and Innocenzo were 'close' as he had put it? Probably . . . she'd never said anything to the contrary, and he seemed to think she'd asked for the young Italian when she was taken to hospital.

But surely he didn't also believe that she had some sort of passionate affair going with Spiro? Well . . . he'd seen what, to him, were definite signs of it, and he'd arrived to find Spiro apparently quite at home with her family.

She wasn't blind; she'd had experience with casual boy-friends and a few who'd been more serious. It seemed to her that Betty was right in thinking Ben was jealous, but if that was so, why had he never made a play for her himself? Because he had this fixation about being responsible for her? Or because he had some notion that an employer shouldn't make passes at his workers? Or because he wanted his men to accept her for what she was, an English student, rather than the girl-friend of the boss?

She sat up in bed, eyes wide. That could be it! Hands

clasped round her knees, she went back over what had passed between her and Ben. She must see him again! He was a reasonable man—most of the time. She'd go to Venice ... she'd book a flight tomorrow! Dad and Betty would think she was mad, and as for Spiro ...

She told him over breakfast. 'Spiro, I'm going to Venice just as soon as I've had my interview with the external assessors at the College. Ben and I had words yesterday and I must talk to him. If you like I'll travel back to London with you before I go. Then it's goodbye. I'm sorry, Spiro.'

'I always knew it was dei Santi,' he said hoarsely, his Italian grammar worse than ever. 'That day in the hospital when they wouldn't let me see you—he'd been with you then, hadn't he, upsetting you? You're in love with him, aren't you?'

'Yes,' she said simply.

'And you think he is serious about you—a pretty little English nobody from—from this?' He waved a hand at the cramped dining-room, the rain-washed garden, the brick works and foundries just visible across the river. 'He is wealthy, Miranda, very wealthy. He has influence in Venice—prestige. He could have almost anyone.'

'I know,' she said, outwardly calm, 'but I'm still going. I'll try for a room at the Signora's. Like it or not, Spiro, I'm going.'

Surprisingly, her father raised no objections. 'As long as you don't miss your interview for your finals,' he said gently. 'You're of age, you have the money for your fare, and if you're sure a phone call won't help, then go. Don't get hurt, pet. Dei Santi seems decent enough, but in my young day it was the chap who did the chasing, not the girl.'

Spiro, unwilling to hang about playing the rejected boy-friend, returned to London immediately. At

Stourley station, boarding the train for Birmingham, he managed to look jaunty and unconcerned to be retracing the previous day's journey, but he left Miranda feeling unpleasantly guilty. She'd caught his expression as the train pulled out, and what was more felt sure he'd applied for the City and Guilds course purely as a means of getting his fare paid to England—and so to her.

She headed for the town centre and a travel agency to see about flights to Venice. She'd never once encouraged Spiro, she thought wearily, so why on earth should she feel guilty about him?

As the plane touched down at Marco Polo Miranda began to feel slightly sick. The compulsion which had brought her back was fading rapidly, and already she was wishing she'd stayed at home. Suppose Ben didn't want to see her? Suppose he'd been on edge in Stourley simply because he could have spent his time more enjoyably elsewhere? Suppose he wasn't jealous at all?

Oh, what was the point in supposing anything? She was here now, and she'd spent a chunk of her earnings getting here. She'd have to see him, and as she could think of no plausible excuse for returning so quickly, she'd tell him the truth—or at least, part of it.

The sun was hot as she carried her case to the quay. No mist this time, she thought, and no Baldassare, either. She stood in the queue wondering if she could share a water-taxi with other new arrivals, when a dark blue launch swished to a halt further along the quay.

Miranda stared. People rushed past her and went down to the taxis, but she stood there with her case at her feet. It *was* the dei Santi launch, and it was Baldassare steering it. But he couldn't have come to meet her, surely? Nobody knew she was coming.

Then a tall, familiar figure leapt ashore and ran up

the steps two at a time. It was Ben, carrying a canvas grip and late for a flight, by the looks of it. He was going away again!

She left her case and ran towards him along the quay. He stopped dead when her saw her. 'Miranda!' He put down his bag and stood quite still as she ran up to him.

'Hello, Ben,' she said breathlessly.

'Baldassare! Wait!' he called. Then he looked down at her and she braced herself for his questions. But he didn't ask her any. Didn't say a word. He just swept her up into his arms and kissed her hard on the mouth.

Her head went back and her lips trembled under his. She was crushed so close to his chest that she felt the heat of his flesh through his thin shirt and her own cotton dress. Then it was over, almost before she had time to enjoy it. He set her back on her feet and said, 'Welcome back, Miranda Brown.'

He hailed a passing porter and sent him inside the airport with his ticket, then turned back to Miranda, picked up her case, and led her to the launch. Baldassare beamed contentedly. 'You are back, Meerandah,' he said, as if her return had never been in question.

'But what about your flight, Ben?' she asked in amazement, 'Shouldn't you be checking in? Where are you going?'

'Back to Venice, with you,' he said calmly, and sat her carefully on a seat as if she were a child's rag doll that needed support in case it fell over. He nodded to Baldassare. 'The showrooms,' he said, and the boatman turned the launch and headed out to the lagoon.

Ben sat next to her and took both her hands in his. 'I don't know what you're doing here, but you've spared me a flight back to England, Miranda. I was going back to Stourley to see you again. If I hadn't been so late I'd have missed you.'

'But *I've* come to see *you*.' she said, somewhat aggrieved. All that soul-searching and agonising and if she'd stayed put he would have been back on the doorstep in no time. 'And another thing—you kissed me!'

'So I did.' He smiled as if he'd enjoyed it. Then he looked at the small hands between his, and said quietly, 'Miranda, when I got back on Friday I went to see Innocenzo.'

'Oh?'

'We had a talk—a long talk. I offered him a loan, telling him it was at your request. I told him that with the sole intention of making him feel even worse about what he'd done to you. He became a bit emotional then, and told me——' He took her fingers and kissed the tips of them, one by one. 'He told me you'd known all along that it was no accident.'

'Oh,' she said for the second time.

'In all our exchanges you never once revealed that, Miranda. In fact you tried desperately to convince me that it was your own fault. At last I began to use my head instead of my heart, and reasoned that if you hadn't liked me just a little you would have thrown the truth in my face and probably shouted for compensation.'

'But Ben——'

'Just a minute. Let me finish—please. I knew all along that something nasty had been planned, although I couldn't believe they'd really intended to burn you. The men ganged up and denied all responsibility, of course, but I *knew*. When I saw you on the floor of the round-house I could have thrown the lot of them in the lagoon, never mind fired them. Then, when I saw what was left of your beautiful hair, and realised how narrowly you'd escaped being killed or disfigured, my one obsession became to keep you out of the works—to keep you safe.'

'You said you "couldn't risk it" when I wanted to go back,' she said, her voice hoarse at the memory of it.

'I meant I couldn't risk anything else happening to you,' he said. 'And I dared not explain further in case you asked me outright for my reasons, because I thought it would upset you terribly if you found out what really happened.'

'I thought you wanted me out of the way in order to pacify the men,' she said quietly.

'The men!' he said scornfully. 'The men are fortunate they still have employment with dei Santi. I made my enquiries, helped by Baldassare, and discovered that the brain behind it all was Innocenzo's. It was he who told the men to pretend they couldn't understand your Italian, and to speak in rapid dialect so that you wouldn't be able to understand them, either. It was he who persuaded the men in the fittings shop to put in the complaint, and it was he who arranged the incident that went wrong—the accident. That shook him. He was so terrified he went home sick—sick with worry, I think. When I found out the part he'd played, then naturally I fired him. What made it rather awkward was that I thought you were attracted to him.'

'You thought that about Spiro, as well.'

'Ah yes, Spiro. He annoyed me because he was always around you, but I didn't give him serious thought until I saw you both at the airport. That staggered me, but I didn't worry unduly because you'd left him here in Venice. Then came the news about the screen. I didn't write or telephone because I wanted to give you the news in person as soon as you'd finished your finals. Then—at the college, I thought you seemed pleased to see me. When, later, I saw Spiro at your father's table feeding Bobby——' He pressed his lips together. 'I was as jealous as hell!'

So Betty had been right. Miranda's heart lifted, while

the launch roared along the staked-out course to where the domes and bell towers of Venice shimmered in the heat haze of midsummer.

They slowed and entered a narrow canal which she knew was a short cut across the city. 'You see, Miranda,' he went on, 'I've been plagued by guilt since the first moment I saw you. Until then I had one ambition—to get the men to accept first foreigners, and then women. Your exhibit in Paris provided me with the ideal opening for achieving that.

'Then, when I saw you at the Signora's all pink and steamy after your bath, the reality of what I was planning to do to you, the way I was going to use you, hit me like a sledgehammer. You seemed so vulnerable, so innocent, so unsuited to face intrigue and rejection, that I seriously considered sending you home without your ever seeing the inside of the glasshouse.

'In the end, of course, I let you start work and hoped for the best. I'd warned the men and I never, ever, dreamed of physical harm coming to you. You can imagine how I felt when you were burned.'

The launch was passing close by Due Ponti, but Miranda didn't mention she was staying there. She'd wanted a long talk, and she was getting it, even if she'd only listened so far. Now, fallen silent, he sat and faced her, still holding her hands, as the launch emerged from the canal.

The holiday season was at its height. Gondolas danced on the waters of St Mark's Basin, *vaporetti* rushed back and forth from the landing stages, the Riva degli Schiavoni was crowded with people. In a broad, triumphant sweep Baldassare crossed the water and halted the vessel at the stone landing stage on the Grand Canal.

Miranda had guessed what they were going to see, and she found she was holding her breath as she stepped ashore outside the showrooms. There, in the window facing the water, was the glass Madonna, set on a swirl of blue silk.

She was beautiful; every detail perfect from the line of her cheek and the curve of her mouth to the smooth sheen of her hair and the creases round the chubby wrist of her baby. The hint of gold in the glass lent depth to the emotions captured in the transparent young face: serenity, radiance, and love for her baby, subtly combining twentieth-century awareness with the timeless strength of the Madonna.

They stood side by side with the water slapping gently beneath the ancient stones. 'You've done it, Benvenuto,' she breathed, 'she's absolutely lovely.'

'We've done it,' he corrected. 'Both of us, Miranda. I was late arriving at the airport because of finishing polishing her and seeing her settled here. I wanted the entire window cleared, except for her.'

Then, belatedly, Miranda noticed the Madonna's setting; the skilful lighting, the dull blue silk, the small engraved card saying: *Dei Santi Madonna. Not for sale.* Finally, her bemused gaze fell to the white plinth on which the Madonna was mounted. Two familiar signatures were there, etched in gold: *Miranda Brown : Benvenuto dei Santi.*

'Armani has seen her,' he went on. 'He said very little, except this: "The Signorina—shall we see her back in the round-house, one day?"'

'That's something, I suppose,' said Miranda warily.

'From Armani, it's the beginning of acceptance. What Armani says today, the rest of the works says tomorrow. I think you've won, Miranda. It may take time, but they'll accept you.'

Her reaction to that was to look up into his face searchingly. Had she imagined that he'd kissed her so fiercely at Marco Polo? And did she dream he'd held her hands and admitted he'd been jealous of Spiro? Was all that a build-up to the announcement that the men might at last accept her? And why were they still standing here?

'Aren't we going inside the showroom?' she asked, puzzled.

'No. There's one more place to go. Baldassare—to San Giorgio Maggiore.'

A little bewildered, she looked back at the Madonna as Ben helped her aboard again. It seemed to her, just for an instant, as if the tranquil gold-tinted face was turned towards her, rather than to the baby.

A moment later she was helped ashore again at the monastery island at the foot of the Grand Canal. Ben turned to her as they crossed to the entrance. 'You did save it for me? The bell tower here?'

'Yes,' she said, mystified. 'I promised I would.'

He took her arm as they entered the quiet white church, but without lingering led her through a door to the left of the altar, and there pressed a bell to summon the lift. A calm, elderly monk in the black robe of the Benedictines greeted Ben as an old friend, and smiled gently over his glasses at Miranda.

'Is there anyone up there?' asked Ben, as they ascended.

'Not at present, Benvenuto.'

'Then could you give us five minutes, alone?'

'I will try,' said the monk, 'but if visitors are impatient . . .' He smiled again, closed the gates of the lift, and left them alone.

'Here is the view,' said Ben, raising an arm and flicking a wrist.

'Oh, Ben! It's lovely!' She walked behind the wall to each side of the tower in turn. There was the sea beyond the Lido, deep blue and hazed on the far horizon; the mysterious islands of the lagoon, green with trees and studded with old buildings; Venice itself, with the many-domed Basilica facing the Piazza; and far away, remote and exquisite, the Alps, soaring up to the smiling heavens as if well pleased to be the backdrop to one of the most spectacular views on earth.

Ben was right next to her, watching her reactions. 'Do you know why I've brought you up here, Miranda?'

'To see the view. And it's really lovely——'

'No.' He took her by the upper arms. 'I've brought you here to tell you that I love you. I've always promised myself that I would propose to the woman I love up here, but you were in Stourley so I knew it would have to be there, instead. Your return today has meant that I can bring you up here, as I've always imagined. I love you, Miranda Brown.'

Eyes enormous, she looked up at him. Then something, perhaps caution, perhaps disbelief, made her ask, 'Is it that you think I'm good with glass?'

For answer, he made a sound that was almost a groan, took her in his arms, and kissed her. His mouth was warm and eager on hers, and as his hands met beneath her shoulder-blades she stood on tip-toe and put her arms round his neck and kissed him back with all the love she'd longed to show for weeks past. Passion flared between them, and she gave herself up to the experience of being in his arms at last, while their bodies swayed together as if they were one and the breath mingled between their lips.

'Does that answer your question?' he asked. 'I've wanted to do that since the first time I saw you, in that ridiculous robe of yours, but for a variety of reasons I forced myself to wait. When we made the Madonna and you gave me that timorous peck on the chin the effort of not making love to you on the spot almost crippled me. But I couldn't do it. I still cherished hopes that the men would accept you for yourself, and I knew quite well they'd be watching. If they'd seen me kissing you then in their eyes you would have been merely the Maestro's girl, and not a glass-maker in your own right.'

He ran his fingers through her hair. 'Oh, Miranda, the times I longed to do that, when it was long and unruly and smelled of roses . . .' He put his lips against it and said, 'The perfume is still the same . . . But you know, the fact that you work the glass like an angel isn't the reason I love you. I love you because you're the most desirable woman I've ever known, because you're warmhearted and brave and unselfish and as honest as the day. The fact of you being good with the glass is just a sort of heaven-sent bonus.'

He held her tight against his chest, and said above her hair, 'I've hardly given you the chance to say a word, have I?' He hesitated. 'You kissed me just now as if—as if——Do you think you could learn to love me, Miranda?'

She seized his hand and held it to her cheek without leaving the circle of his arms. 'I shan't have to do much learning. I've loved you for ages, Benvenuto.'

'Will you marry me?' he asked promptly.

'Yes.' All the reservations she'd had about their different backgrounds vanished in an upsurge of joy.

'You'd agree to live here—in Venice?'

'Where else?' she said, beaming. 'We'll get married here as well, if you like.'

'The dei Santis have always married here, it's true,' he conceded, 'and my father would be pleased to see the Marriage Cup used once again.'

'And the Madonna can be in church to watch us,' said Miranda.

'We'll bring your family over, and——' The bell sounded. Someone was waiting to come aloft.

'Let's go somewhere quiet, where we can start kissing again,' she suggested.

He laughed out loud at that. 'When I went dashing off to the airport I never imagined I'd hear you say that to me within the hour,' he said. 'Let's go to my island.'

'But I'm staying at Signora Gaspari's.

'Stay with me, instead,' he said, his hands on her waist.

They could hear the lift ascending. 'One more kiss before we go,' he murmured, tilting her face up to his.

Above them the sea breeze whispered through the timbers supporting the great bells, while down below the restless water lapped at the quay, and a burly, grey-haired figure awaited their return.

Take 4 best-selling love stories FREE
Plus get a FREE surprise gift!

Six exciting series
for you every month...
from Harlequin

Harlequin Romance·
The series that started it all

Tender, captivating and heartwarming...
love stories that sweep you off to faraway places
and delight you with the magic of love.

◆

Harlequin Presents·
Powerful contemporary love
stories...as individual as the
women who read them

The No. 1 romance series...
exciting love stories for you, the woman of today...
a rare blend of passion and dramatic realism.

◆

Harlequin Superromance®
It's more than romance...
it's Harlequin Superromance

A sophisticated, contemporary romance-fiction
series, providing you with a longer,
more involving read...a richer mix of complex plots,
realism and adventure.

Harlequin American Romance™

Harlequin celebrates the American woman...

...by offering you romance stories written about American women, by American women for American women. This series offers you contemporary romances uniquely North American in flavor and appeal.

◆

Harlequin Temptation™

Passionate stories for today's woman

An exciting series of sensual, mature stories of love...dilemmas, choices, resolutions... all contemporary issues dealt with in a true-to-life fashion by some of your favorite authors.

◆

Harlequin Intrigue

Because romance can be quite an adventure

Harlequin Intrigue, an innovative series that blends the romance you expect... with the unexpected. Each story has an added element of intrigue that provides a new twist to the Harlequin tradition of romance excellence.

Harlequin Books·

PROD-A-2

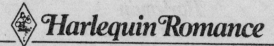
Harlequin Romance

Coming Next Month

2821   ROAD TO LOVE Katherine Arthur
A free-lance photographer happens upon a Clark Gable
look-alike and a chance to pay off her debts. So when he takes
off across America in his shiny silver semi, little does he know
she's along for the ride.

2822   THE FOLLY OF LOVING Catherine George
Times are tough, and it seems foolhardy for an Englishwoman
to turn down a famous actor's marriage proposal. But he broke
her heart eight years ago. So hasn't he done enough already?

2823   WINTER AT WHITECLIFFS Miriam Macgregor
The owner of Whitecliffs sheep station in New Zealand puts
his ward's tutor on a month's trial, and all because he thinks
she's after his half brother. But if he knew where her true
interests lay...

2824   THE SECRET POOL Betty Neels
A nurse's holiday in Holland seems the perfect escape from the
critical appraisal of a certain Dutch doctor—until he tracks her
down, having decided she's perfect for a particular job after all.

2825   RUDE AWAKENING Elizabeth Power
A computer programmer, accused by her suspicious-minded
boss of stealing company secrets, finds herself kept prisoner by
him until she can prove her innocence.

2826   ROUGH DIAMOND Kate Walker
The volatile attraction a young Englishwoman felt for her rebel
from the wrong side of the tracks is reignited years later—along
with the doubts and confusion that drove them apart.

Available in March wherever paperback books are sold, or
through Harlequin Reader Service.

In the U.S.
P.O. Box 1397
Buffalo, N.Y.
14240-1397

In Canada
P.O. Box 603
Fort Erie, Ontario
L2A 5X3